Birthday Surprises

· Ten Great Stories to Unwrap ·

EDITED BY

Johanna Hurwitz

A Beech Tree Paperback Book
New York

The authors included in this anthology and Morrow Junior Books support and encourage children's enjoyment of writing and literature. All of the authors' royalties as well as the publisher's profits from the sale of this book will be donated to The Writing Project of Teachers College, Columbia University, and the National Writing Project of the University of California, Berkeley.

The text type is 13-point Weiss.

Printed in the United States of America.

The Library of Congress has cataloged the Morrow Junior Books
edition of Birthday Surprises *as follows:*
Birthday surprises: ten great stories to unwrap/edited by Johanna Hurwitz.
p. cm.
Contents: The special powers of Blossom Culp/Richard Peck—No such thing/Ann M. Martin—Birthday box/Jane Yolen—Don't be an Uncle Max/David A. Adler—What the princess discarded/Barbara Ann Porte—Hattie's birthday box/Pam Conrad—The birthday of Madeleine Blore/Karla Kuskin—Victor/James Howe—Promises/Ellen Conford—The empty box/Johanna Hurwitz.
ISBN 0-688-13194-8
1. Birthdays—Juvenile fiction. 2. Children's stories, American. [1. Birthdays—Fiction. 2. Short stories.] PZ5.B486 1995 [Fic]—dc20 94-26640 CIP AC

5 7 9 10 8 6 4
First Beech Tree Edition, 1997
ISBN 0-688-15295-3

Contents

Introduction

Some years ago, I got the idea for an interesting project: the same plot would be offered to several children's book writers to see how each author handled the same basic idea. After all, I've always felt that all writers use and reuse a limited number of plots. It's the different style, characters, setting, voice, and point of view that each writer brings to the telling of a story that makes it unique.

This project of mine was not so original. Among a collection of old books, I discovered a wonderful anthology of stories by famous British writers all using the same plot (*Mr. Fothergill's Plot,* Oxford University Press, 1931). Though it had been published years before I was born, it was still fun to read. More recently, several mystery authors were asked to write conclusions to the same tale (*The Perfect Murder,* edited by Jack Hitt, HarperCollins, 1991). There is even a magazine called *Thema,* published four times a year, that aims to stimulate creative thinking by having writers and poets address a single designated theme in each issue.

I thought for a while and came up with the following premise, on which this book is based: *A child (boy or girl) receives many gifts on his or her birthday. However, on opening the presents, one beautifully wrapped package is found to be empty.*

Before I submitted this to other authors, I tested myself. How many different ways could I write the story? Within a few hours I had thought of a dozen variations. Good, I decided. If I could think of so many, then so could other people.

Letters were sent off to writers of children's books all across the United States and even across the ocean. Most wrote back saying that they were intrigued by the idea. However, some were too busy with their other writing and did not have time to meet this new challenge. Author Betsy Byars wrote to say that she had written a chapter in a forthcoming book, *McMummy,* entitled "The

Empty Birthday Present." I was surprised when I got her letter. Yet I shouldn't have been. In fact, perhaps there are other "empty birthday boxes" in literature of which I am not aware.

I'm sure you will be as amazed as I was to see how each of the contributors to this collection has interpreted and built on my premise. For, while it is possible to receive two identical birthday presents, it is impossible for two writers to produce the exact same story. Even though you know in advance that each story is about an empty box, each story—like the box it is about—still contains a surprise.

Some of the stories in *Birthday Surprises* will make you laugh. Others may make you cry. They will all make you think. There are contemporary stories and stories with a historical twist. There is a modern fairy tale and there is a bit of fantasy. There is even a poem. The stories have been written in the first or the third person. My own story is epistolary, which is a fancy way of saying "in the form of letters." And just like in everyday life, some of the birthdays are being celebrated by girls and some by boys.

I'll bet you could use your imagination to write an alternate version of this situation. If a birthday box is empty, what is the reason? I think every person who reads this book can give still another slant, another voice, to this story. Life is full of surprises, and you'll probably be surprised at all the possibilities this tale can hold.

And who knows, perhaps you will want to come up with a different plot of your own with which to challenge and amuse your friends and classmates.

The Special Powers of Blossom Culp

· Richard Peck ·

My name is Blossom Culp, and I'm ten years old, to the best of my mama's recollection.

I call 1900 the year of my birth, but Mama claims to have no idea of the day. Mama doesn't hold with birthdays. She says they make her feel old. This also saves her giving me a present. You could go through the courthouse down at Sikeston, Missouri, with a fine-tooth comb without turning up my records. But I must have been born because here I am.

Since Mama is hard to overlook, I will just mention her now. She doesn't know her birthday either but claims to be twenty-nine years old. She has only three teeth in her head, but they are up front so they make a good showing. Her inky hair flows over her bent shoulders and far down her back. Whenever she appeared in daylight down at Sikeston, horses reared. Mama is a sight.

But she is a woman of wisdom and wonderful when it comes to root mixtures, forbidden knowledge, and other people's poultry. We could live off the land, though the trouble is, it's always somebody else's land. Like many of nature's creatures, Mama goes about her work at night. Get your corn in early, or Mama will have our share. Plant your tomatoes up by the house, or Mama will take them off you by the bushel. She likes her eggs fresh, too.

A moonless night suits her best; then off she goes down the hedgerows with a croaker sack flung over her humped shoulder. But nobody's ever caught her. "I can outrun a dawg," says Mama.

It was another of her talents that got us chased out of Sikeston. To hear her tell it, Mama has the Second Sight. For ready money she'll tell your fortune, find lost articles, see through walls, and call up the departed. She can read tea leaves, a pack of cards, your palm, a crystal ball. It doesn't matter to Mama. But because Sikeston was a backward place and narrow in its thinking, her profession was against the law. So her and me had to hotfoot it out of town two jumps ahead of a sheriff's posse.

Mama said that fate was mysteriously leading her to our next home place. But we'd have hopped a freight in any direction. Aboard a swaying cattle car, Mama grew thoughtful and pulled on her long chin.

"The farther north we get," she said, "the more progressive. Wherever we light, you'll be goin' to school." She shifted a plug of Bull Durham from one cheek to the other. If Mama had ever been to school herself, she'd have mentioned it. About all she can read is tea leaves.

"I been to school before, Mama," I reminded her. Down at Sikeston, I'd dropped into the grade school occasionally. Though when I dropped out again, I wasn't missed.

"I mean you'll be goin' to school regular," Mama said. "I don't want the law on me—believe it."

So when at last we came to rest at the town of Bluff City, I knew school was in my future without even a glimpse into Mama's crystal ball. I well recall the day I strolled into the Horace Mann School in Bluff City, wearing the same duds from when me and Mama had dropped off a cattle car of the Wabash Railroad.

"Yewww," said many of the girls in the school

yard, giving me a wide berth. It was no better inside. I was sent to the office of the principal before I had time to break a rule. She was a woman tall as a tree named Miss Mae Spaulding.

"Oh dear," she said, looking down at me, "we're going to have to find you a comb."

I was small for ten but old for my years. Miss Spaulding seemed to grasp this and assigned me to fourth grade. She took me there herself, shooing me on ahead like a chicken. The teacher, name of Miss Cartwright, took a gander at me and said, "Oh my stars."

"Perhaps you'd have a spare handkerchief to loan Blossom," the principal said to Miss Cartwright over my head.

I wiped my nose on my sleeve and noticed all the eyes of fourth grade were boring holes in me. The boys' eyes were round with amazement. The girls' eyes were mean slits.

"I guess we had better find Blossom a seat," Miss Cartwright said as Miss Spaulding beat a retreat out the door.

A big girl reared up out of her desk. She wore a bow the size of a kite on the back of her head. "She'll not be sitting next to me!" she sang out, and flopped back.

Her name turned out to be Letty Shambaugh, and once again I didn't need Mama's Second Sight to see I had met an enemy for life.

Miss Cartwright cleared her throat and said, "Boys and girls, we have a new class member. I will ask her to introduce herself."

I looked down the rows of fourth grade, and they looked capable of anything. Still, I stood my ground. "My name is Blossom Culp," I said, "and I hail from down at Sikeston, Missouri."

Letty Shambaugh twitched in her seat. "Hillbillies," she hissed to the girls around her, "or worse."

"Me and Mama have relocated to Bluff City on account of her business," I said.

"Ah," says Miss Cartwright behind me, "and what...business is your mother engaged in?"

"Oh well shoot," I says, "my mama is well known for her herbal cures and fortune-telling. She can heal warts, too. There's gypsy blood in our family."

Letty Shambaugh smirked and so did the girls around her. "Ah," says Miss Cartwright. "And are you an only child, Blossom?"

"I am now," I said. "I was born one-half of a pair of Siamese twins, but my twin had to be hacked off my side so I alone could live."

"She lies!" Letty Shambaugh called out, though all the boys were interested in my story.

By now Miss Cartwright had pulled back to the blackboard and seemed to be clinging to the chalk tray. "You may take your seat, Blossom." She pointed to the rear of the room.

I didn't mind it on the back row, but as the weeks passed, the novelty of going to school every day wore thin. My reading wasn't up to fourth-grade standard either. Still, when we had to rise and read aloud from a library book, I did right well. Holding a book before me, I'd tell a story I made up on the spot.

"Lies, lies," Letty would announce, "nothing but lies!" Still, Miss Cartwright was often so fascinated, she didn't stop me.

Then one day she told us that Letty would be having her birthday party on school time. "It is not usual to have a birthday party in class," Miss Cartwright said, "but we are making an exception of Letty."

People were always making an exception of Letty, and her paw was the president of the Board of Education. "Mrs. Shambaugh has very kindly offered to provide a cake," Miss Cartwright said, "and ice-cream punch."

At recess that day I was in the girls' rest room,

which has partitions for modesty. From my stall I eavesdropped on Letty talking to the bunch of girls she rules: Tess and Bess, the Beasley twins; Nola Nirider; and Maisie Markham.

"Now shut up and listen," Letty told them. "I am looking for some first-rate presents from you-all for my birthday. Don't get me any of that five-and-dime stuff."

I was so interested in Letty's commandments that I leaned on the door of my stall and staggered out into full view.

"Oh there you are, Blossom," Letty sniffed. "Since you do nothing but tell lies and snoop, I'll thank you not to give me a present at all. You are a poor girl and can't afford it. Besides, I want nothing from the likes of you."

The bell rang, and they all flounced off like a gaggle of geese. But Letty turned back to fire a final warning. "And don't let me catch you spying on us again, Blossom."

You won't, I said, but only to myself.

I sat up that night, waiting for Mama to come home. We'd taken up residence in an abandoned structure over past the streetcar tracks. It must have been midnight before Mama came in and eased her croaker sack down.

Then she busied herself shaking out everything

she'd harvested from nearby gardens. From the look of some of it, she'd detoured past the town dump. It was late in the season, so all there was to eat was a handful of pale parsnips.

"Well, Mama, I've got me a problem," I told her. "A stuck-up girl at school is having a birthday party, and I mean to give her a present like anybody else."

Mama surveyed her night's haul. "See anything here you can use?"

She held up a lady's whalebone corset straight off the trash heap and busted beyond repair. Besides, it wouldn't go halfway around Letty. The rest of the stuff was worse, except for a nice hatbox only a little dented with the tissue paper still inside. I reached for it. Mama only shrugged, picking between two of her three teeth.

The school days droned on, but I kept my wits about me. In one of my read-alouds, I went too far. Holding up a library copy of *Rebecca of Sunnybrook Farm,* I told the class about the time my mama came across the severed head of a woman and how Mama could identify the murderer with her Second Sight.

"A pack of lies!" Letty bawled out, "and disgusting."

"That will do, Blossom," Miss Cartwright said in a weary voice. So after that, I had little to occupy myself with but to lie low and snoop on other people's business.

On the afternoon of Letty's party, a cake was wheeled in as large and pink as Letty herself. The classroom was stacked with tastefully wrapped presents, and no learning was done in fourth grade that afternoon. Miss Cartwright hung at the edge while Letty was the center of attention, where she likes to be.

We played some games too childish to interest me, but I managed three slabs of cake and copped an extra slice to take home to Mama. Then it was time for the presents.

"Oh heavens, you shouldn't have!" says Letty, her pudgy fingers fluttering over the vast heap. "Land sakes, I don't know which one to open first."

"Start with this one." I nudged the hatbox toward her with the toe of my shoe. I'd dressed it up with a bow I found in the school yard and some gold star stickers I'd come across in a teacher's desk.

Miss Cartwright was standing by. Though strict, she sometimes eyed me sympathetically, though it might only have been pity. "Yes, Letty," she said. "Start with Blossom's present."

So Letty had to. She shook the box but heard nothing. She lifted off the lid and ran a hand through the tissue paper. "But there's nothing in it!" she gasped, shooting me a dangerous look.

Some of the boys snickered, but the girls just pursed up their lips. "Oh dear," Miss Cartwright remarked. Now Letty had turned the hatbox upside down. The tissue paper dropped out and with it a small note I'd hand lettered. She read it aloud:

To Letty,

Since I am too poor to buy you a present, I will share with you my own personal Gift.

Believe it,

Blossom Culp

Letty glanced longingly at her other presents. "What is this so-called personal Gift of yours, Blossom?"

"Just a little demonstration of the Special Powers I inherited from my mama," I replied.

Letty shook a fist at me. "Blossom, you aren't going to ruin my party by showing off and telling lies!"

"For example," I said, cool as a cucumber, "before you even open up your other presents, I can tell what's in them with my Inner Eye. It's a Gift, and I have it down pat."

The girls were about to turn on me, but a boy said, "Then do it."

I could read the card on Nola Nirider's. "Now you take Nola's present." I pointed it out. "No, I don't want to touch it. Just give me a minute." I let my head loll. Then I let my eyes roll back in my head. It was a ghastly sight, and the class gasped. In a voice faint and far-off I said, "Within the wrappings, I see...a woman! She is a dainty creature cut in two at the waist!" I let my eyes roll back in place and looked around. "What did I say?"

Letty was already tearing open Nola's present. She pulled out a dainty china powder box in the shape of a lady. It was in two parts. The lid was the upper half. The boys blinked, and the girls looked worried.

Reading the card on Maisie's present from afar, I said, "Now you take that one from Maisie Markham." And back flipped my eyes, and my head bobbed around till it like to fall off. "Deep within that fancy package," I moaned weirdly, "is a sealed bottle of apple-blossom toilet water—retailing at seventy-nine cents. I sense it with my Inner Nose."

Letty ripped open the box, coming up with that

selfsame bottle of toilet water. "How am I doin'?" I asked the class.

It was the same with Tess's brush-and-comb set and Bess's four hair ribbons in rainbow hues. My eyes rolled back so often, showing my whites, that I thought I'd never get them straight in their sockets.

By now Letty sat sprawled in a heap of wrapping paper, the tears starting down her red face. She was clouding up and ready to squall and had to stand up to stamp her foot. "You have ruined my party with your showing off, Blossom. I knew you would, and you have!" She pounded out of the room before she even got to any presents from the boys, which was just as well. The other girls followed her out as usual.

It's true. I stole Letty's thunder and her party, too. Now I was left with the boys, who showed me new respect, unsure of my special powers. But then the bell rang, and they trooped out, taking final swipes at the remains of the birthday cake.

"One moment, Blossom," Miss Cartwright said before I could make it to the door. "Could it be as you say—that you have...unearthly powers? Or could it merely be that you eavesdropped in the rest room often enough to hear those girls telling each other what they were giving Letty—and then you added that business with your eyes?"

Her chalky hand rested on my shoulder. "No, don't tell me," she said. "I don't want to know."

I was ready to go, but Miss Cartwright continued. "It has not taken you long to make a name for yourself at Horace Mann School. You will never be popular. But I have hopes for your future, Blossom. You will go far in your own peculiar way."

And I only nodded, as it's never wise to disagree with a teacher. Then she turned me loose, and I went on my way.

No Such Thing

· Ann M. Martin ·

On the morning of his eighth birthday, Marco woke up early. Birthdays meant presents, and he knew a lot of them were waiting downstairs. For days Marco had watched them pile up.

"This is torture," he had complained to his father a week earlier. "Can't I open one now? Or maybe two?"

"Marco," replied his father, "if you start opening your presents now, you won't have any left for your birthday. That would be real torture."

"Bullfrogs," Marco had said. And he had marched upstairs to his room. He flopped on his bed. He had a long talk with his dog. Puddles had never answered him, but Marco felt sure he could talk anyway. He thought all animals could talk. Just because he hadn't heard them didn't mean it couldn't happen. But that's what grown-ups seemed to believe. Even his big brothers. Marco let out a sigh. Most grown-ups had no imagination whatsoever. Marco vowed not to be like them when he grew up. He would be like Grandpa Leslie. Now Grandpa had an imagination. A big one. So what if he was absentminded, too? Marco could live with that.

"Hey, Puddles!" exclaimed Marco as he leaped out of bed. "Today is my birthday! I'm eight years old. Finally."

Marco had been waiting for this day since his seventh birthday. He was sure that now his brothers, who were twelve and fifteen, would treat him with a little more respect.

Plus, of course, there were those presents piled up on the table in the living room. Fourteen in all. Marco had counted them six times the day before. And the biggest box was from Grandpa Leslie. Marco just knew it would be a great gift. Not a sweater (which Grandma Ruth was apt to send) or a savings bond (which Auntie Mary was apt to send—and all wrapped up in a box, too, so that it looked like a real present, instead of just a piece of paper). No, Grandpa Leslie would send something really terrific. On Marco's seventh birthday he had sent a butterfly hatcher. And it had worked. Marco had hatched live butterflies and watched them fly off into the woods behind his house.

"Come on, Puddles!" cried Marco. "Let's go downstairs." And he flew down the steps in his pajamas with Puddles at his heels.

But when he reached the kitchen, his mother said, "Happy birthday, Marco. Now go back upstairs and get dressed. You know the rules."

"Bullfrogs," muttered Marco as he returned to his room.

Fifteen minutes later, Marco was dressed and seated at the kitchen table. Around him were his parents and Jacob and Robert. Jacob and Robert were his brothers, the teasers. However, Marco was halfway through his scrambled eggs, and they hadn't teased him once. Either they were being nice and respectful because Marco had finally turned eight, or they were saving up their teasing for something big.

"Mom? When can I open my presents?" asked Marco. "Can I please open them right after breakfast?"

"Yes, you may," she replied. "In fact, you

may open one right now. Here." Marco's mother handed him a long flat box. Marco opened it in a flash. Inside was Auntie Mary's savings bond.

When the breakfast dishes had been cleared away, Marco and his family gathered in the living room. Marco's father got out the video camera. "I want to record this for posterity," he said. He said that on every big occasion.

"Can I start opening now?" Marco asked.

"Just let me get a glass of water," said Jacob.

"I have to go to the bathroom first," said Robert.

"More coffee, dear?" Marco's father asked his mother, and he headed for the kitchen.

Marco sighed. When his family had gathered once again, he didn't wait a moment longer. He reached for the present on the top of the pile and tore into it. It was a sweater from Grandma Ruth. A pale blue sweater with chicks and bunnies on it. Grandma Ruth had absolutely no idea how old Marco was. But after the horrible sweater came a mystery book from his godfather, a new set of colored pencils from Robert, a collection of practical jokes (the whoopee cushion was the best one) from Jacob, and lots of toys from his parents.

At last only Grandpa Leslie's package remained. Marco had not even taken it out of its brown wrapping. Grandpa Leslie had decorated the mailing carton with sticker pictures and drawings of cats and dogs. Marco had not wanted to ruin that. But now he lifted up the box. "It's awfully light," he said, and he felt a bit disappointed. It certainly couldn't be the woodworking set he'd hinted that he wanted.

Marco pulled the brown paper off the package. He opened the carton. He peered inside. The box was empty. No present. Not even any crumpled-up newspaper or bits of Styrofoam. Nothing.

"What is it?" asked Jacob and Robert, leaning over to see.

"The box is empty," said Marco in a whisper. He wanted to cry. Why would Grandpa Leslie do that to him? Didn't he know the empty box would embarrass Marco? Didn't he know Jacob and Robert would tease him about it? Didn't he love Marco?

Two towns away, Grandpa Leslie was eating his breakfast and thinking of Marco. He was wondering if Marco had opened the fabulous woodworking set. He thought about calling him but realized he hadn't fed his cat yet. Monkey's bowl was empty.

"Or *did* I feed you?" Grandpa asked Monkey. He couldn't remember. "Maybe you ate your breakfast already. You do eat awfully fast." Grandpa scratched his head. When he did, he knocked his glasses to the floor. "Oh, *there* you are!" he exclaimed. "I've been looking all over for you." Grandpa put his glasses on. Then he fed Monkey. "Better to be fed twice than not at all," he said to himself. "And now," he went on (Grandpa talked to himself a lot), "I must call Marco. Where is the phone?"

For Grandpa's seventy-fourth birthday Marco's family had given him a cordless phone. Grandpa thought it was a wonderful gift. The only problem was that he could rarely find it. He never remembered where he had set down the receiver. Often he had to wait for someone to call him so he could follow the sound of the ringing to the lost phone. Now Grandpa went on a search for the phone. He looked on his messy desk. He found a glove he had lost, but no phone. He looked on the messy kitchen table. He found the hammer he had lost, but no phone. He looked in a messy closet. Of course he did not find the phone, but he did find Marco's birthday present.

"How can this be?" cried Grandpa. "I mailed

this off last week, didn't I?" Grandpa scratched his head again. He thought hard. He remembered buying the woodworking set. He remembered wrapping it up and tying a ribbon on it. He remembered buying a special carton to mail the gift in. And he remembered wrapping the carton in brown paper, decorating it for Marco, and taking it to the post office. "The only thing I forgot," he said, "was to put the present inside first."

Grandpa ran upstairs to his old telephone. He dialed Marco's number. The line was busy.

"Bullfrogs!" said Grandpa. "There is just one thing to do."

Grandpa grabbed the present. He threw it into the back of Dinky, his rumbly, jumbly old car. Then he clapped his hat on his head, called goodbye to Monkey, and hopped into the car. "I can get to Marco's in an hour if Dinky holds up," he said.

Grandpa Leslie turned the key in the ignition. He stepped on the accelerator. *Sputter-sputter-putt-putt-putt* went Dinky. "Come on," said Grandpa. "Come *on*."

Putt-putt-vroom went Dinky.

"Good car," said Grandpa, and he backed slowly down his driveway and eased into the street. Then Grandpa hit the gas. Dinky jumped forward.

(Dinky's top speed was thirty-five miles per hour.)

"Okay," said Grandpa. "We're on our way. Here I come, Marco."

Back at Marco's house, Marco was sitting in the living room among his presents. He had phoned Auntie Mary to thank her for the savings bond, and Grandma Ruth to thank her for the bunny sweater, and his godfather to thank him for the book. Now he examined his set of practical jokes. The vanishing ink looked interesting, but Marco's mind was on other things.

Why had Grandpa Leslie embarrassed him by sending him an empty package? Jacob had started laughing about that and hadn't been able to stop. Now Robert came into the room, sat beside Marco, and said, "Ha! Grandpa must love me more than he does you. He sent me a video game for my birthday. Remember?"

"Of course I remember," muttered Marco.

Jacob grinned. "Not an empty box," he went on. "A completely empty box. Hmm. Now what could that mean? That he doesn't love you at all? That—"

"Oh, shut up," said Marco.

Marco jumped to his feet. He ran out of the living room. Then he ran through the hallway and out the back door. He stood in the yard for a few moments. "Puddles!" he called. "Hey, Puddles! Want to take a walk with me?...Puddles?"

Marco felt quite lonely. His brothers were big teases, Grandpa Leslie had hurt his feelings, and now Puddles wouldn't even keep him company. So Marco set off for the woods all by himself.

"Won't you come home, Bill Bailey? Won't you come home?" sang Grandpa Leslie. Grandpa just loved to sing. Especially when he was behind the wheel in Dinky. He sang silly old songs, and he had taught them all to Marco.

When Grandpa finished "Bill Bailey," he started another one. "Put on your old gray bonnet with the blue ribbons on it, and we'll hitch old Dobbin to the sleigh."

Grandpa sighed. He was trying to enjoy the trip, but he felt terrible about Marco's present. Plus, Dinky was creeping along more slowly than usual. Grandpa patted the dashboard. "Please, Dinky. Just a little more energy, okay? Maybe you could speed up to thirty miles per hour. I don't think that's asking too much."

But Dinky held steady at twenty-five.

"Daisy, Daisy, give me your answer, do," sang Grandpa. Then he murmured, "I'm coming, Marco."

Marco was wandering through the woods. He passed the tree in which Jacob and Robert had built a fort. He passed the stream where he and Puddles looked for minnows and crayfish. Finally he came to the large flat rock where he sometimes liked to sit and think. So he sat and thought.

While he was sitting, a blue jay swooped down. It perched on a branch near Marco's head and squawked at him.

"Hi, blue jay," said Marco. "Well, you will never guess what happened to me today. It's my birthday. My *eighth* birthday. And my grandfather sent me an empty box."

"Hmphh. Empty. There's no such thing as empty," replied the jay. "That box was full of the sky, the wide blue sky. And the sky is where birds fly."

Marco's mouth dropped open. "Did you say something?" he asked the jay. "I mean, did you just say what I think you said?"

But the jay had already soared off.

Marco shook his head. He really was not sure

the jay had spoken. Nevertheless he thought, I knew it! I knew animals could talk. Wait until I tell Grandpa Leslie. When I'm not so mad at him, that is.

Marco slid off the rock. He walked through the woods again. He didn't stop until he saw an owl. It was nestling into a hole in a tree trunk.

"Hey, owl," called Marco. "Guess what. Today is my birthday, and my grandfather sent me an empty box."

The owl was high above Marco's head, so Marco stood on his tiptoes and listened hard. And he was pretty sure he heard the owl reply, "Why, there's no such thing as empty. That box was full of the nighttime, dark and starry. And nighttime is the best time for owls. What a wonderful gift." With that, the owl pulled himself all the way into the hole and closed his eyes.

"Owl! Hey, owl! Did you just talk?" called Marco.

The owl did not reply. So Marco thought about the box. His grandfather had sent him the wide sky and the starry nighttime. Maybe it wasn't such a bad gift after all.

Grandpa Leslie crept along the winding road to Marco's house. Behind him trailed a long line of cars and trucks. The drivers were beeping their horns. *Honk, honk! Beep, beep, beeeeeeep!*

"Hey, buddy! Speed it up!" shouted one driver, leaning out of his window.

"Pull over and let us pass!" called another.

Grandpa didn't hear them. "Nothing could be finer than to be in Carolina in the mor-or-orning," he sang.

Marco left the owl's tree. He wandered back toward the brook. A rabbit hopped in front of him. "Hey, rabbit," said Marco, and he told him about his birthday present.

The rabbit would not let Marco come near him, but Marco thought he heard him say, "There's no such thing as empty. That box was full of memories, memories your grandfather wants you to have."

"Really?" replied Marco. He was feeling a lot better and decided that maybe it was time to go home. His parents might be worried about him.

Marco set off again. But he stopped short when a squirrel darted up a tree and began to chatter at him.

"Did you hear about my birthday present?" Marco asked him.

And he was positive he heard the squirrel say,

"The empty box? Silly boy. There's no such thing as empty. That box was full of love, your grandfather's love. Now go on home. Right away."

Marco took the squirrel's advice. He began to run. He ran until he reached the edge of his backyard.

Grandpa Leslie had just turned into Marco's driveway when Dinky sputtered to a stop. The car would not go an inch farther. So Grandpa set the parking brake and got out of the car. He was about to take the woodworking set out of the backseat when he heard someone call, "Grandpa! Grandpa!"

There was Marco. He was running across the yard, looking excited and sounding breathless.

"Grandpa, thank you for the present!" cried Marco as he dashed toward his grandfather. "At first I thought it was a mean trick, but now I understand what you sent. The memories and love parts are the best. Oh, and I finally heard the animals talk. Thank you, Grandpa Leslie. Thank you!"

Grandpa had no idea what Marco was shouting about. None whatsoever. But he didn't want to spoil Marco's excitement. He stepped away from Dinky. Then he held out his arms. "Happy birthday," he said. "I'm glad you liked your present."

"It was the best one I ever got," replied Marco.

Birthday Box

• Jane Yolen •

I was ten years old when my mother died. Ten years old on that very day. Still she gave me a party of sorts. Sick as she was, Mama had seen to it, organizing it at the hospital. She made sure the doctors and nurses all brought me presents. We were good friends with them all by that time, because Mama had been in the hospital for so long.

The head nurse, V. Louise Higgins (I never did know what that *V* stood for), gave me a little box, which was sort of funny because she was the biggest of all the nurses there. I mean she was tremendous. And she was the only one who insisted on wearing all white. Mama had called her the great white shark when she was first admitted, only not to V. Louise's face. "All those needles,"

Mama had said. "Like teeth." But V. Louise was sweet, not sharklike at all, and she'd been so gentle with Mama.

I opened the little present first. It was a fountain pen, a real one, not a fake one like you get at Kmart.

"Now you can write beautiful stories, Katie," V. Louise said to me.

I didn't say that stories come out of your head, not out of a pen. That wouldn't have been polite, and Mama—even sick—was real big on politeness.

"Thanks, V. Louise," I said.

The Stardust Twins—which is what Mama called Patty and Tracey-lynn because they reminded her of dancers in an old-fashioned ballroom—gave me a present together. It was a diary and had a picture of a little girl in pink, reading in a garden swing. A little young for me, a little too cute. I mean, I read Stephen King and want to write like him. But as Mama always reminded me whenever Dad finally remembered to send me something, it was the thought that counted, not the actual gift.

"It's great," I told them. "I'll write in it with my new pen." And I wrote my name on the first page just to show them I meant it.

They hugged me and winked at Mama. She tried to wink back but was just too tired and shut both her eyes instead.

Lily, who is from Jamaica, had baked me some sweet bread. Mary Margaret gave me a gold cross blessed by the pope, which I put on even though Mama and I weren't churchgoers. That was Dad's thing.

Then Dr. Dann, the intern who was on days, and Dr. Pucci, the oncologist (which is the fancy name for a cancer doctor), gave me a big box filled to the top with little presents, each wrapped up individually. All things they knew I'd love—paperback books and writing paper and erasers with funny animal heads and colored paper clips and a rubber stamp that printed FROM KATIE'S DESK and other stuff. They must have raided a stationery store.

There was one box, though, they held out till the end. It was about the size of a large top hat. The paper was deep blue and covered with stars; not fake stars but real stars, I mean, like a map of the night sky. The ribbon was two shades of blue with silver threads running through. There was no name on the card.

"Who's it from?" I asked.

None of the nurses answered, and the doctors both suddenly were studying the ceiling tiles with the kind of intensity they usually saved for X rays. No one spoke. In fact the only sound for the longest time was Mama's breathing machine going in and out and in and out. It was a harsh, horrible, insistent sound, and usually I talked and talked to cover up the noise. But I was waiting for someone to tell me.

At last V. Louise said, "It's from your mama, Katie. She told us what she wanted. And where to get it."

I turned and looked at Mama then, and her eyes were open again. Funny, but sickness had made her even more beautiful than good health had. Her skin was like that old paper, the kind they used to write on with quill pens, and stretched out over her bones so she looked like a model. Her eyes, which had been a deep, brilliant blue, were now like the fall sky, bleached and softened. She was like a faded photograph of herself. She smiled a very small smile at me. I knew it was an effort.

"It's you," she mouthed. I read her lips. I had gotten real good at that. I thought she meant it was a present for me.

"Of course it is," I said cheerfully. I had gotten

good at that, too, being cheerful when I didn't feel like it. "Of course it is."

I took the paper off the box carefully, not tearing it but folding it into a tidy packet. I twisted the ribbons around my hand and then put them on the pillow by her hand. It made the stark white hospital bed look almost festive.

Under the wrapping, the box was beautiful itself. It was made of a heavy cardboard and covered with a linen material that had a pattern of cloud-filled skies.

I opened the box slowly and...

"It's empty," I said. "Is this a joke?" I turned to ask Mama, but she was gone. I mean, her body was there, but she wasn't. It was as if she was as empty as the box.

Dr. Pucci leaned over her and listened with a stethoscope, then almost absently patted Mama's head. Then, with infinite care, V. Louise closed Mama's eyes, ran her hand across Mama's cheek, and turned off the breathing machine.

"Mama!" I cried. And to the nurses and doctors, I screamed, "Do something!" And because the room had suddenly become so silent, my voice echoed back at me. "Mama, do something."

• • •

I cried steadily for, I think, a week. Then I cried at night for a couple of months. And then for about a year I cried at anniversaries, like Mama's birthday or mine, at Thanksgiving, on Mother's Day. I stopped writing. I stopped reading except for school assignments. I was pretty mean to my half brothers and totally rotten to my stepmother and Dad. I felt empty and angry, and they all left me pretty much alone.

And then one night, right after my first birthday without Mama, I woke up remembering how she had said, "It's you." Not, "It's for you," just "It's you." Now Mama had been a high school English teacher and a writer herself. She'd had poems published in little magazines. She didn't use words carelessly. In the end she could hardly use any words at all. So—I asked myself in that dark room—why had she said, "It's you"? Why were they the very last words she had ever said to me, forced out with her last breath?

I turned on the bedside light and got out of bed. The room was full of shadows, not all of them real.

Pulling the desk chair over to my closet, I climbed up and felt along the top shelf, and against the back wall, there was the birthday box, just where I had thrown it the day I had moved in with my dad.

I pulled it down and opened it. It was as empty as the day I had put it away.

"It's you," I whispered to the box.

And then suddenly I knew.

Mama had meant *I* was the box, solid and sturdy, maybe even beautiful or at least interesting on the outside. But I had to fill up the box to make it all it could be. And I had to fill me up as well. She had guessed what might happen to me, had told me in a subtle way. In the two words she could manage.

I stopped crying and got some paper out of the desk drawer. I got out my fountain pen. I started writing, and I haven't stopped since. The first thing I wrote was about that birthday. I put it in the box, and pretty soon that box was overflowing with stories. And poems. And memories.

And so was I.

And so was I.

Don't Be an Uncle Max

• David A. Adler •

I held out my arms and said, "Ma, you don't understand." And she didn't. "There's a school rule. If a teacher checks homework, you do it. If she doesn't, you don't."

"Joanne," Mom asked, "could you please tell me where you learned that rule?"

"Is that one of those restorable questions?" I asked.

"It's a rhetorical question," Mom said, "not restorable."

Well, you don't have to answer that kind of question, so I didn't.

"Listen," I said. "The first time she gave us history homework, I did it. I even looked in the book so some of the answers would be right. But when

Mrs. Taylor checked the homework, she didn't even read what I wrote. And she didn't put a mark on it. So I decided to let her keep looking at that homework until she did read it."

"Are you telling me that you've been showing her the same paper since September?"

I didn't answer. I was hoping that was another one of those restorable questions.

"Well?" my mother asked loudly.

I nodded.

Mom's eyes opened wide, like the time she found worms and snails in my lunch box.

"It's the middle of January. You haven't done your homework for four months!"

She was wrong, so I corrected her.

"It's only January twelfth. January has thirty-one days, so the middle would be January sixteenth at noon."

Mom looked ready to shout again, but she didn't. That's because I was right.

She quietly counted to ten. She does that sometimes when she thinks she's getting too angry. It's a problem she has.

"...seven, eight, nine, ten."

Mom looked at the note Mrs. Taylor had sent home and started counting again.

"One, two, three,...seven, eight, nine, ten."

Mom took a deep breath and then said, "Well, from now on your father and I will check your homework, and you can be sure we'll read it."

No, they won't. I'll write sloppy.

"For the next week, there won't be any dessert in your lunch."

Mom gives me homemade brownies, but I call them burnties. I tried feeding the burnties to the pigeons. They wouldn't eat them either.

"And you're having a birthday soon. If we get another deficiency letter, you won't get any presents."

I waited. Mom had something else to say and I knew what it was. "You're just like your Uncle Max."

Max is Mom's brother.

I'd love to be like Uncle Max. He doesn't like to shave, so he grew a beard. I probably don't like to shave either, but I can't grow a beard. I'm too young, and I'm a girl.

Mom said, "Uncle Max didn't do homework and now look at him."

Uncle Max travels to lots of great places. In November he sent me a postcard from Alaska. "Dear Jo," he wrote. "I work in a general store and we sell just about everything except generals. What I love most here are the people, the sleds, the scenery, and the snow. Love, Max."

Mom says Uncle Max can't keep a job, that he always gets fired. That's why he keeps moving. She says he's irresponsible. Dad says other things about Uncle Max, but I'm not allowed to repeat them.

Uncle Max sends me the best gifts. He once sent me a bird's nest that the birds didn't need because they had moved. He sent me cat bones, skin that a snake had crawled out of, and snails that people eat, only I didn't.

I told Uncle Max that I couldn't have a pet because my dad is allergic. He wrote to me, "Don't worry, Jo. I'll take care of it." And he did.

Two months later he sent me a big box. Inside was an old birdcage he had found and painted gold. Taped onto the perch was a cardboard letter *J* that he had colored blue. I call him Tweets. He's my pet blue jay.

Uncle Max trained Tweets before he sent him to me. Tweets doesn't fly out even if I leave the cage door open. And at night, when I'm pretending to be asleep, he's real quiet and pretends to be asleep too.

"Just sit right here where I can watch you," Mom said, "and do your homework."

I put my books on the kitchen table, next to Mom's pink and blue alphabet beads. It's for her business. She makes baby bracelets with the baby's name inside. I've told her she can write anything. Babies can't read. But she still tries to spell their names right.

I had history homework, all about George Washington. He had false teeth made of wood. I had math homework and science homework, too. I did it all. I wondered if children in Alaska had to do homework.

The next morning, before I went to school, Dad held my hands and looked into my eyes.

Here it comes, I thought. And it did.

"Don't be an Uncle Max," he told me.

Dad hadn't shaved yet, and he had burned toast crumbs and butter on his lip and chin. He looked like a grizzly bear.

I would love to be an Uncle Max. I'd love to live in Alaska and not do any homework. I didn't tell Dad that, but that's what I was thinking.

For the next few days Mrs. Taylor actually read my homework. Then she began calling on me in class. It was horrible and had to stop. So I called out a few times and yelled, "Ooh, ooh!" Mrs. Taylor got real angry at me. She refused to call on me anymore.

That was just what I wanted.

Then, one night, Dad came home with a large

package. He kept it behind his back until he was sure no one was watching. He hid it in the front closet. I watched his reflection in the glass on one of my baby pictures. I would make a good spy.

Dad went upstairs, and I went to the closet. The box was wrapped in happy-birthday paper, so I knew it was for me. It was big but not too heavy. I tried to slide the paper off, but there was tape all over. I shook it, but nothing rattled. Clothing. Yuck!

I heard Dad coming downstairs. I ran to the kitchen and pretended to be doing homework.

At dinner I said, "Please," and "Thank you," and all those good-manners words. Mom likes that. After dinner I spoke to her. "If you want to know what I want for my birthday, it's a spy kit."

Mom didn't say anything. But she heard me.

I did homework all week. And sometimes I even looked in the book. So I know some of the answers I wrote were right.

Then, two days before my birthday, a delivery company brought a box to our house. It was wrapped in brown paper. It was from Uncle Max. The delivery woman gave it to Mom. The box was addressed to her, but I knew it was for me. Mom took it upstairs.

After dinner I looked for the box. I wasn't going to open it. I just wanted to know how heavy it was and if it would rattle when I shook it. I couldn't find the box. Mom is pretty good at hiding things. And I couldn't find the spy kit I hoped Mom had bought for me.

The box was about the size of one of those small television sets. I could stay up all night and watch that television in my room.

Or maybe Uncle Max had sent me a bug. Not the kind that crawls, but the kind that spies use to listen to other people's conversations.

A snake. Uncle Max knows I want one. And Dad isn't allergic to snakes because they don't have fur or feathers.

In school the next morning I said "Ooh, ooh" a few times. I jumped out of my seat. I waved both hands up and down and then in large circles.

Mrs. Taylor said, "I appreciate your enthusiasm, but I'm not calling on you until you learn to raise your hand properly."

That was just what I wanted. Now I was free to think about what Uncle Max had sent me.

A shortwave radio.

A long-wave radio.

Alaskan gold.

Crocodile teeth.

Boxing gloves.

A calculator watch that makes telephone calls. Diana has one. It makes sounds like a Touch-Tone telephone and can actually call someone. But it doesn't talk to them.

On the morning of my birthday, we all ate breakfast together. In my family, on birthdays we always have cake for breakfast. Mom lit the candles on my cake. She and Dad sang "Happy Birthday" to me.

The cake was gooey and chocolate. Just the way I like it. I ate two big pieces.

Then came the presents.

"This is from me," Dad said, and gave me the box that didn't rattle. I opened it. A dark blue sweater with fake pearls sewn on. Yuck.

"Thank you, Dad. It's beautiful."

"And this is from me," Mom said, and gave me a small box. I knew it wasn't the spy kit because that comes in a big box. I opened it. A periscope. Neat. Now I could do some serious spying.

"Thanks, Mom."

There were other presents but nothing great.

Then Mom gave me the box from Uncle Max.

"Don't open it yet," Mom said. "There's a note."

Mom reached over and took the envelope off the top of the box and tore the envelope open.

The box was light.

"Dear Jo," Mom read. "Happy birthday. I'm leaving Alaska soon. I wanted to get you something special and expensive, but I needed lots of money for plane fare to Brazil. That's where I'm going next. I decided to send you one of the things I'll miss most when I leave this beautiful place."

I shook the box. It didn't rattle.

I tore off the brown paper. The box lid was taped closed, and the tape wouldn't come off. Dad cut it with a knife and then gave the box back to me.

I opened the box.

What!

The box was empty.

I looked at my parents and then in the box again. It was a little wet.

I turned the box upside down and shook it. A small piece of paper fell out, another note from Uncle Max. He wrote, "This box is filled with Alaska snow and lots of love."

Wow!

Only Uncle Max would think of sending me snow from Alaska.

Isn't he great? (That's a restorable question.)

I read the note again.

Uncle Max also sent me lots of love. Sometimes I really need that. I taped the box closed again so none of the love would fall out.

What the Princess Discarded

· Barbara Ann Porte ·

When Alice received her invitation to the princess's birthday party, she began right away to think about what she could take as a present. She knew the princess already had nearly everything, or at least everything money could buy. The princess didn't get presents like the rest of us do—only on birthdays and holidays. She got presents daily. They arrived for her in the mail, by special delivery, and by private messenger service. They filled up her bedroom, piled up in the hallways, and overflowed the palace closets.

The queen frequently brought up the need for a larger palace, or maybe one consisting of only closets, or, perhaps, one palace for the princess and another for her parents. A single palace often seemed too small for even just the three of them, not to mention so many servants, ladies-in-waiting, butlers, pages, valets, and footmen. Plus, alas, there was this: The princess was often extremely unpleasant. Her manners were atrocious. She took almost anything—a cold, bad weather, brussels sprouts at dinner—as a good excuse for rudeness. Even at her age, she threw tantrums.

Her parents, the king and queen, didn't like to complain. Having borne and raised her, they worried that her behavior was in some way their fault. The queen recalled a distant cousin who'd behaved a lot like the princess. Well, she'd been banished, but those were the old days. Banishment was no longer in style. "And quite rightly so," the queen told the king, but she sounded doubtful as she said it.

The king recalled a tantrum of his own, thrown right on the steps that led to the palace. Well, he'd been only three at the time and had received a royal spanking. Spankings, too, were out of style now. "And rightly so," the king told the queen, but he sounded doubtful as he said it.

On truly awful days, though, the king and queen looked at each other and said, "Everything cannot be our fault. The princess must be held accountable for some things." Well, of course they should have told this to the princess, but they did not care to incur her wrath and tried, for the most part, just to keep out of her way, with plenty of space between them, which isn't *that* hard when you are king and queen, living in a capacious castle.

But getting back to Alice—in her presence, the princess was on her best behavior. Well, she had to be. Alice was neither a relative nor a servant. Alice could leave when she liked and always did at the first signs of petulance on the part of the princess. Therefore, in Alice's company, the princess took pains to be pleasant, which goes to show she did know the difference.

The princess liked having Alice around. Well, who wouldn't? Alice was even-tempered and considerate, with a talent for thinking up new things to do, activities and games that were never boring. Also, the very fact she couldn't be bullied intrigued the princess, so used to those who toadied and curried and gave in to her every whim. As far as the princess could see, Alice had only one flaw, a strawberry birthmark that covered a large part of her neck.

Naturally, Alice would have preferred not having the birthmark, but she wasn't about to let it ruin her life or force her into wearing turtlenecks all of the time or wraparound scarves. Also, she'd been told the mark was likely to disappear on its own one day, and, even if it didn't, as her neck grew larger, the mark would *seem* smaller.

The princess actually liked it. She thought it had the good effect of setting off her own clear skin's perfection rather nicely. She invited Alice to the palace frequently, including to every party that she gave. The princess, in turn, went to all of Alice's parties and gave the most extraordinary presents.

Two years ago, for instance, she'd sent ahead a troupe of entertainers—a retinue of dancing girls and fiddlers to accompany them. Well, it was very nice to see them dance and to listen to the band, but when the party ended and the guests went home, the retinue remained, needing to be fed and put to bed. Alice's parents couldn't begin to afford so many dinners, not to mention pillows, linens, and mattresses. Sending the troupe back would have seemed rude. Finally Alice's mother located a performing arts company in Peru and sent the troupe there. The company was glad to have them, and they were pleased to go, having heard the climate was healthy. Transportation was expensive, but as Alice's mother often said afterward, "Some things are worth it."

The following year, the princess's birthday gift to Alice was a zebra. "Much better than a horse. It's more rare and amusing to look at," the princess said.

"It's a good thing she didn't give you an elephant," Alice's mother said, thinking of the food bills.

"Or a tiger," said Alice's father, thinking of lawsuits. But Alice thought only of the zebra, in cramped quarters, lonely, so far from its natural habitat. So, once again, her parents scraped together sufficient money, this time to send the zebra off to Africa, a one-way ticket to the Serengeti Plain in Tanzania. That was when they discovered it's sometimes cheaper sending a crowd than a zebra. Still, whenever Alice thought of that zebra now, eating wild grasses and romping with friends, it seemed worth it.

"Sure, worth it, but it didn't come out of your allowance," Alice's mother said. But she smiled as she said it, because Alice was such a lovely child in nearly every way, so polite, and turning out as well as any parents ever could have hoped. Well, Alice's parents would have liked to see her strawberry mark go away, or at any rate fade or get smaller. Still, they told each other, "Just look at the princess. A flawless complexion, but her heart's in the wrong place." They wondered what Alice saw in her.

It may have been this: On the one hand, Alice tried always to look on everyone's good side and overlook another person's faults as much as possible. Perhaps she'd learned this from experience. And on the other hand, even a girl as sensible as Alice is likely to have her head turned at least a little by the pomp and perquisites accruing to a royal friendship. Alice liked lunches at the castle, trying on crowns, being helped into and out of her coat by ladies-in-waiting. Parties at the palace were scrumptious—double-chocolate cakes, every flavor of ice cream, zillions of multicolored balloons, and all those splendiferous presents, so astonishingly wrapped, to be undone, held up, and admired. No wonder Alice thought so hard, trying to decide what she could possibly give that would befit the upcoming occasion. Finally her mind was made up. She knew what to do.

Every afternoon for the next several weeks, and sometimes in the evenings, Alice retired to a little woodshed behind her house, from which her parents could hear sounds of hammering and sawing, humming and whistling, and, sometimes, Alice singing. As the sounds grew increasingly harmonious, and also, believing as they did in rights of privacy, even for children, Alice's parents left her alone, didn't ask questions, and never once peeked. By the day of the party, Alice's present for the princess was ready, and so was Alice.

Alice walked to the palace holding the present in both hands very carefully, so as not to drop it. It was square-shaped and not very large, about the size of a pound box of chocolate bonbons. It was neatly gift wrapped in shiny red paper, with a white and red polka-dot bow. Alice arrived at the party precisely on time. Even so, there were dozens of guests before her, and dozens more followed behind, some of them bringing dozens of presents. You can imagine how long it took opening them. There was hardly any time for games or even just chitchat. Well, there were lots of balloons, ice cream, and a chocolate cake in the shape of a crown. When the princess blew out all her candles, Alice wondered what the princess could be wishing for that she didn't already have.

Maybe she wished for more friends at her party.

Considering her manners, it wasn't too surprising that, except for Alice, all the guests were relatives, or those whose jobs depended on the king and queen, or subjects hoping for some future royal favor or feeling that they needed to demonstrate their loyalty. Others sent regrets and tokens of appreciation.

The princess received two hundred pairs of white lace tights, for instance; one hundred pairs of patent leather shoes, in five different colors, most the wrong size; fifty argyle sweaters; twelve dozen bears, including a real dancing one; nearly as many dolls with real hair and eyes that opened and closed; not to mention all those brightly colored wind-up clowns and monkeys, with moving parts, that tipped their hats and bowed so cunningly.

"Do you know, when I was her age, my favorite toy was a wooden spinning top," the king told the queen as they both looked on.

"My favorite present when I was her age was a copy of the book *The Kind-Hearted Prince,* with color illustrations," the queen told the king. They both smiled a bit wearily, wondering what the princess could do with so many presents and wherever would she keep them. They hadn't even all been opened yet. Alice's was last.

The princess tore off the paper and bow, and tossed them atop what was by now a very steep heap in one corner. She didn't even read the card enclosed, and that was her misfortune. It might have saved considerable misunderstanding. Instead, the princess stared in disbelief at her present.

It was a box, an empty box. Actually, it was an extraordinarily beautiful box, of fine fruitwood, wonderfully carved, and decorated with a circle of exotic dancers, fiddlers fiddling, and a few zebras. The princess peered closer, thinking perhaps she'd missed something. She even turned the box upside down and shook it. Nothing fell out. It was definitely empty.

"Humph," said the princess. She stamped one foot and tossed the box across the room. Fortunately, it landed undamaged on top of that same heap of discarded wrappings. How ungrateful, the princess thought, glaring at Alice—after all the nice presents I've given her in the past. Well, we'll just see what she gets next year!

As for Alice, she looked on, perhaps surprised but not at all perturbed. She knew how fine a gift she'd made and also knew that she could always make another. In fact, going home, that's exactly what she decided to do.

"This next one is sure to be even better," she told herself. "Now I have experience." Her parents could not have been more pleased, seeing their daughter so happy with her new hobby, whatever it was.

Meantime, back at the palace, the servants were busy sorting gifts and cleaning up. The empty box, discarded as it was among the ribbons and wrappings, was set out, along with the rubbish, to be hauled away in the morning. That was how it happened that an underpaid seamstress, on her way home, took a quick look through the trash and saw it there. "It's certainly beautiful," she told herself. "And who knows, it may come in handy someday." When you are poor enough, everything has some value. She took it with her and gave it to her son, who had few toys and all of them either hand-me-down or homemade. He was happy to have such a nice box.

At first he kept it on a shelf and admired it. He enjoyed the fruitwood fragrance it gave off. Once he went so far as to touch his tongue to the box and taste it, but it tasted flat, like paper, and he never tried that again. He did like to hold the box in his hands, though, and stroke it, enjoying the smooth feel of the wood. Eventually, he ran his hands everywhere over that box, inside and out. And that was how, even lacking the card that had come with it, the one the princess had thrown out, he discovered its secret.

Hidden beneath the box lid was a lever, and when the boy pressed it, music began to play—the crystal-clear tones of a flute; the rich, dulcet sounds of a lute; and in the background, wondrous high notes, as though sung by a diva. Nor was that all, because by the time the music stopped, the boy had discovered a tiny key set alongside the lever. When the key was turned, the music began all over again. The moving parts of the box remained hidden. The boy was enchanted. And why not? It wasn't *any* music box. It was the first one ever, or at least in that part of the world. No wonder the princess hadn't known what it was. Alice had only just invented it.

The story doesn't end here, though, by a long shot. Alice grew up. So did the boy and the princess. Year by year, the princess grew more ornery, finally avoided by everyone, except the hired help paid to look after her. She did wind up with a prince. The marriage was an arranged one. It couldn't have been a more perfect match. The prince behaved the same as the princess—so we know how that turned out!

Alice was not invited to the wedding. She was much too busy, though, to notice. Having discovered the pleasures of inventing, she'd gone on to new projects. She showed her work in science fairs and was interviewed by the media. She became famous. How proud her parents were of her.

As for the boy, he became quite a musician. Listening had trained his ears. With time on his hands and few toys to distract him, he'd practiced tapping out rhythms and whistling. Later he'd taught himself to make his own musical instruments, woodwinds and strings, cut from trees in the forest, pipes and lyres, lutes and drums, some he had no names for. He played them all to his heart's content, composing as he went. It made him very happy, and that, of course, made his mother happy, too.

Eventually the musician met Alice—at a science fair. It's not surprising she was there, but what about him? Well, it's a scientific fact: Inventors are frequently musical, and musicians are often inventive. This musician liked keeping up with new technology. As it happened, on the day he visited, Alice was exhibiting, for old times' sake, the second music box she'd ever made. It was a lot like the first one. The musician stared, amazed, then struck up a conversation with Alice. One thing led to another. They soon fell in love and were married.

Time passed. One day as the musician was helping Alice button up her smock, he kissed her on the neck and said, "I really like your birthmark. I'm glad you have it. In case some evil genie should ever turn you into a toad or a princess and try to hide you, I could always find you. I'd know you by your mark and turn you back."

Alice smiled. She hardly noticed anymore she had one, much less hoped for it to go away or even fade, though it did seem smaller now. She had more important matters on her mind—children, for instance, twin girls and a boy. They all three were inventive, and definitely musical, and turning out as well as any parents ever could have hoped. Well, occasionally one or another of them had a tantrum, acted up, behaved rudely. At such times, Alice told tales. A favorite of hers began:

"Once upon a time there was a princess who had everything to make her happy, including a wonderful music box." Alice invented new middles as she went. The conclusion was always the same.

"See, that princess held happiness in both her hands. Then, just like that, she threw it out. Don't you be that way," Alice warned her children, and for a long time after, they weren't. So, if this family didn't live happily ever after, it did live well and in harmony most of the time. And that's a true story.

Hattie's Birthday Box

· Pam Conrad ·

The sign stretching across the ceiling of the nursing home's rec room says HAPPY ONE HUNDREDTH BIRTHDAY, SPENCER McCLINTIC, and on the wall in bright numbers and letters it says JULY 5, 1847 TO 1947. Spencer McClintic is my great-great-grandfather, and our whole family is coming to celebrate.

Momma and I got here early because Momma wanted me to help her blow up balloons and tack up the decorations before everyone arrived. She says now that the war is over and most everyone is back home and rations are a thing of the past, we're going to *really* celebrate.

But Grandaddy's nervous. He sits in his chair by the window, rubbing his hands together and asking my mother over and over, "Now who-all is coming, Anna?"

And she keeps reciting the list of everyone who's coming, and he ticks them off on his fingers, but before she's even through, he asks impatiently, "But is Hattie coming? My baby sister? Are you sure she's coming?"

"Hattie's coming, Grandaddy. Don't you worry. Hattie will be here."

Momma doesn't hear, but I hear him. He mumbles, "Oh, no, oh, no, not Hattie. She's gonna skin me alive."

I pull up a stool near Grandaddy. "Don't you like Aunt Hattie, Grandaddy?"

"Oh, I love her to pieces," he answers. "But she's gonna have my hide. Last time I saw Hattie, she was a bride of sixteen, heading out in a wagon with her new husband to homestead in Nebraska. And I did a terrible thing, a terrible thing."

All the decorations are up, and now that Momma's sure everything is all set, she tells me to stay with Grandaddy and keep him calm while she runs home to get the cake and soda.

But there is no way to keep Grandaddy calm. "What'd you do that was so bad, Grandaddy? What was it?"

"Well, if that gal comes in here with a shotgun and shoots me full of pellets, you tell the sheriff I deserved it, you hear? I had my long life, a hundred years, and I prob'ly deserve to be blown to kingdom come."

I watch Grandaddy wringing his hands and tapping his slippered feet nervously. He keeps glancing out the window to the road outside, like he's waiting for some old lynch mob to come riding over the hill. This is the story I finally got out of him.

It had been a warm May morning in 1873, and Grandaddy's sister Hattie McClintic Burden was a new bride ready to set out for a life on the distant, promising plains of Nebraska. The sun hadn't quite risen yet, and she and her new husband, Otto, were loading the final things into the wagon. While it was a happy occasion in that Hattie and her husband were heading out for a new life, it was also a sad day, because no one knew when they'd ever see them again. Grandaddy, who was a young man at the time, didn't know it would be seventy-four years before he would finally see her. But no one ever knew that back then. No one knew how long it would be before they saw each other or if they would ever see each other at all. There were no telephones, no airplanes, just the U.S. mail, slow but reliable, carrying recipes for pumpkin bread and clippings of hair from new babies, and sad messages of deaths.

The night before Hattie and Otto left, everyone had tried to smile and be happy for them. There was a combination going-away party and birthday party for Hattie, who was just sixteen. Everyone brought special gifts—blankets and lanterns and bolts of cotton, a pair of small sewing scissors, a bottle of ink, and even a canary in a shiny cage.

My grandaddy, who was then a young man of twenty-six, had stewed and brooded. He had been ten years old when Hattie was born, and she had always been his favorite. More than once he had carried her out into the barn on crystal-clear nights to show her a calf being born. He had taught her to swim in the cool spring. And he had chased away the young boys when they had first started to come sniffing around. His heart was breaking that his little sister was going away, and he had wanted to give her the most special gift. The best gift of all. So she would always remember him and know how much he had loved her.

He would have given her a gold necklace, or a bracelet with diamonds, or earrings with opal jewels, but it had been a rough year, with a few of the cattle dying in a storm and a few others lost to a brief sickness. He had no money, nothing to trade, no real gift to give her. Not knowing what the gift would be, he had lovingly hammered together a small wooden box and carved her initials in it, thinking that whatever it would be, it would be about this size.

It was at the party that night that he realized there was nothing to give her and he concocted his tale. Finding her alone at the punch bowl, Spencer had clasped Hattie's small shoulders in his rough hands, looked straight in her face, and lied boldly.

"I got you something special, Hattie, something so special I think you'd better not open it right away. I want you to just hold on to the box, and don't open it unless times get hard, not unless things get to be their very worst, you hear me? And it will see you through."

Hattie had looked at him with such love and trust. He memorized her face, the same small face she had turned to him when a birth-wet calf had finally struggled to its feet, or when he had carried her out on snowy nights to turn her tongue to the swirling night sky. Her face was soft with love, and he knew she must have thought his gift was something precious that she could sell if crops failed or some other disaster happened. But he lied, he lied.

So that morning before the sun rose, he helped Otto hook up the team to the wagon, and once Hattie was high on her perch beside her husband—looking for all the world like a little child playing farmhouse—my young grandaddy had slipped the sealed and empty wooden box into her lap and backed away. He waved goodbye and never saw her again.

Until today. Aunt Hattie's flying in from Nebraska with cousin Harold and his wife, Mary. Since she was sixteen, Hattie has never set foot off Nebraska soil.

"I meant to finally buy her something to put in the box, I really did," Grandaddy keeps saying. "I thought that as soon as things got a little better, as soon as I had a little money, I'd buy those earrings or that necklace and send it right off to her, explaining everything. But then I don't know. Soon I got married myself, and then there were my own children, and Hattie just never mentioned it in any of her letters." Grandaddy groans and lowers his head into his upturned hands. "Oh, mercy, Hattie's coming."

People are starting to arrive now, and the room is filling with children, laughter, and presents. Many of the people are my relatives who live right nearby, and a few came up from Jersey and Washington, people I'd normally see on holidays and such but never all together like this in one place.

And Grandaddy won't even look at them. He just gets up and walks slowly to another seat far from the window. Out the window I see an airport taxi pull up.

I post myself behind Grandaddy and watch. His hands are trembling more than usual, and I can tell he's not paying attention as little babies are brought to him to kiss and my father keeps taking flash pictures of him with everybody.

Suddenly a hush falls over everyone. Even the littlest children grow wide-eyed and still. The name "Hattie" is whispered across the room, like prairie wind over the flute of a stovepipe.

"It's Hattie."

"Hattie's here."

"Hattie!"

I put my hand on Grandaddy's shoulder. "Don't worry, Grandaddy. She'll have to get through me first."

Grandaddy takes a deep breath, and his shoulders slump. He doesn't turn toward the door. He just waits in the silence that falls over the room. We can hear footsteps, Harold's and Mary's, and Hattie's. They stand in the doorway with Hattie in the middle, as though they support her, but when she sees Grandaddy sitting with his back to her, she gently withdraws her arms from them and comes toward us.

She doesn't look like she could swat a fly, and she's not packing a shotgun. The tiny thin net on her hat trembles as she takes tiny steps toward us. "Spencer?" she says softly.

"Grandaddy," I say more sharply, poking him in the arm. "Grandaddy, it's Hattie."

He turns then, ready to meet his Maker, I guess, but I'm right there, right next to them, able to see both their faces, and there is nothing but pure love, pure and powerful and undeniable love.

"Why, Spencer, they told me you were an old man." She holds out her hands to him, and he takes them.

Tears stream down his cheeks and drip from his chin. "But no one told me you were still such a pretty young lady," he says. Still lying, my grandaddy.

"Oh, Spencer, Spencer," she says, "there's been

too much time and space." And I watch her gather him into her skinny little arms, and he lays his face against her shoulder. No one in the room is breathing. Then all of a sudden, one of the cousins starts to clap, and everyone, one at a time, joins in, until everyone is laughing and wiping tears, patting Grandaddy on the shoulder, and hugging Hattie.

I'm not about to leave Grandaddy's side. If she's ever going to give him the business about the empty box, I want to hear it. Someone brings her a chair and sits her down right next to him, and no one stops me so I sit down between them right at their feet. And then I notice it. On her lap is a small wooden box, and the lid is off. Delicately carved into its varnished top are the initials HMcB. She holds the box in her hands, and I can see the varnish worn dull in spots where her fingers touch and must have touched for years.

Grandaddy sees it, too, and groans. "Oh, Hattie, do you hate me? Can you ever forgive me?"

"Forgive you for what?"

"For the empty box."

"Forgive you? Why, Spencer, it was the best present I've ever gotten."

"An empty box?" Grandaddy is stunned.

"It wasn't an empty box. It was a box full of good things."

"How d'you figure that?" Grandaddy asks.

"Well, I put it in a safe place, you know. First I hid it under the seat in the wagon, and when we finally got our soddy built, I had Otto make a special chink in the wall where I hid it and where it stayed for years. And I always knew it was there if things got really bad.

"Our first winter, we ran out of food, and I thought to open the box then and see if it would help us, but there were kind neighbors who were generous with us, and I learned to let people be neighborly.

"And then one summer we lost our whole crop in a prairie fire, and I thought of the box, but Otto was sure we could make it on our own, and I learned to let him have his pride. Then when our son drowned, just out of despair I almost opened it, but you had said to open it only if things got their worst, and I knew I still had my daughter, and there was another baby already stirring in me.

"No matter how bad things got, Spencer, they never got their worst. Even when Otto finally died a few years ago. Your box taught me that."

"But you did open it." He points to the box, open and empty in her lap.

"I opened it when I knew I'd be seeing you. I always thought maybe there'd be a brooch or a gold stickpin or something." Hattie smiles. I can almost imagine her with her open face turned up to a snowy sky. She laughs. "I was going to wear it for you!"

"I always meant to fill it, Hattie—"

"Hush now," she says. "They're bringing your cake."

And sure enough, Momma's wheeling over a metal table that has a big iced sheet cake on it. Hattie slips the cover back on her empty box and places it on the floor beside her feet, beside me. I stand to get out of the way of the rolling table and take the box.

Grandaddy and Aunt Hattie hold hands while everyone sings "Happy Birthday." Their hands are like old wisteria vines woven into each other. I hold the empty box. I bring it to my face. I look inside. Nothing. It is empty. And then I smell it. At first I think it smells like wood, and then I smell all the rest—a young farmer's stubbornness, a pioneer mother's sorrow, and a wondrous wild and lasting hope.

The Birthday of Madeleine Blore

· *Karla Kuskin* ·

Remember the birthday of Madeleine Blore?
She was nine.
She had had eight
great birthdays before.
And each was a triumph
with presents galore,
cake, cookies, and singing,
loud laughing and more,
all making dear Maddie feel grateful
and pleasant
EXCEPT for the absence
of one special present.

What *was* it?
What was it?
Well what *could* it be?
If you asked,
there was silence from Madeleine B.
She only would say
that her birthdays were fine.
One through seven were heaven.
Eight was divine.
And now she was thrilled,
simply thrilled,
to be nine.

But then in a whisper
that no one could hear,
she would add, "Oh, if only
that present were here,"
as she brushed from her cheek
a small, sparkling tear.

On the day of this birthday of Madeleine Blore,
a package arrived at a little past four.
First a ring of the bell,
then a rap at the door
and the next thing we knew

it was there
on the floor.
There was something about it—
the paper?
the size?
that filled us with wonder
and dazzled our eyes.
It was bigger than bigger
than bigger by half.
Did it hold a small house
or a little giraffe?
And the wrapping was special,
it looked to my eye as if it was wrapped
in a piece of the sky.

First Madeleine opened a puzzle from Jess,
then a bracelet from Jool,
then a sweet set of chess.
She loved every gift
and she thanked every giver.
The arrows were perfect, she said,
with the quiver.
She admired the old-fashioned
miniature store
and at last she approached
the big box on the floor.

She took off the paper
and opened the lid
and the strangest thing happened
as soon as she did.
When she opened the lid
and she peered deep inside,
her very brown eyes opened up very wide
and all of us leaned in to see what was there.
But there wasn't a thing
except empty-box air.

Madeleine smiled her most magical smile.
She took a deep breath
and she held it awhile.
And then with the teeniest, tiniest shout,
she reached in
and pulled all the emptiness out.
And she hugged it,
this nothing that no one could see
(except for the nine-year-old
Madeleine B.).
"Just look at the shape," she cried,
"look at the drape.
It is finally mine,
AN INVISIBLE CAPE.

Isn't it marvelous?
Isn't it clever?
It's just what I've wanted
for ever
and ever."

THEN
in less than a second,
or possibly two,
she wrapped the cape 'round her...

and vanished from view.

Victor

• James Howe •

I guess I do believe in miracles. I never did, but then one happened to me. See, I thought I was going to die. I don't mean to sound dramatic about it or anything, but that's the truth. Everybody else thought so, too. My mom was crying all the time, and my dad was all the time trying not to. I don't get that about guys. I mean, I was only twelve then, so I guess you could say I wasn't a man yet, but I'd learned a long time ago I shouldn't cry. Well, the way I feel about it is this: If you found out your kid was going to die, it would be pretty stupid *not* to cry. Don't you think?

Anyway, I couldn't say to my dad, "Come on, let it all out, man," because I couldn't talk. Everybody else could. My relatives would come and hold my hand and say stuff like, "Lookin' good, Cody." Then they'd turn to my mom or dad, whichever one was on duty, and—keep in mind, they're still holding my hand here—they'd say, their voices all dry and cracked like old city sidewalks, "I can't bear to see him lying here like this. It just breaks my heart." And then they'd put my hand back on the bed, soft as a peach they didn't want to bruise, and reach for my box of Kleenex and wipe their noses and hurry up their goodbyes, and they'd be out of there. Pretty soon, I'd be alone with my mom or dad and the sound of the IV dripping and the TV playing across the hall. And pretty soon after that, the room would start getting dark, and my mom or dad would bend over me to kiss my cheek and say, "Sweet dreams, Cody." And another day would come to an end.

When I was first in the hospital, everybody brought flowers or comic books or boxes of chocolates. But, seeing as how there was no way for me to enjoy any of these things and my mom was telling everybody she was getting fat eating all the chocolates, my visitors began showing up with nothing but sad faces. And then more time passed than anybody had figured on; it seemed I was going to keep on living, even if I wouldn't exactly have called it that, and they all remembered they had their own lives to live.

It started getting pretty lonely. A few of my friends still came around. Max. I could always count on him coming by at least a couple of times a week. And of course my mom and dad. They were there, one or both of them, every day. But there were long stretches of time when it was just me and the ceiling. Now here's the amazing thing about that ceiling—and this is important, even though I know it's going to sound crazy: I got to thinking that that ceiling was a place. You know, a real place you could go to. In your mind, anyway. It was made up of acoustical tiles; you know the kind, those squares with all the little holes and jig-jaggy lines in them. Well, if you've got nothing else to look at all day long, you'd be surprised how much you can see in all those little holes and jigs and jags. Rivers and lakes. Hills and valleys. Highways. Back roads. After a while, I started dividing up the whole ceiling (or the part of it I could see, anyway; I couldn't move my head unless somebody moved it for me) into villages and cities. I called all of it the Land Above.

Pretty soon I was telling myself stories about

the people who lived in the Land Above. The funny thing is, I never gave them names. I don't know why. I've always liked to write stories, and one of my favorite parts is coming up with the characters' names. But for some reason I imagined these people right down to their moles, but I never knew what to call them.

There was one person who lived in the Land Above I need to tell you about. He was old. And he was very strong—not strong like a weight lifter but solid strong, like an oak tree. And strong in his heart and mind. He was the one all the other people looked up to, the one they turned to when they were in trouble. He never spoke until he'd thought a long time, and then he always knew just the right words to say. His face was kind but as full of holes and jig-jaggy lines as that ceiling. Sometimes at the end of the day, before the nurses had gotten around to turning on the overheads and the light in the room was pale and sleepy, I could make out his face on the third tile down, two to the left. I decided that's where he lived. Third tile down, two to the left.

Nobody knew about the Land Above but me, of course. Nobody knew I had company even when I was alone. I guess to everyone else I was a sad case. Now that I think of it, I guess I was.

Then one night long after my parents had kissed me and wished me sweet dreams, after their footsteps had carried them away from me and the elevator's *ting* had signaled that they were on their way back to what was left of the other parts of their lives, just as I was drifting near sleep, I heard a voice say, "Don't get many visitors anymore, do you?"

It was a man's voice, soft and deep as a forest, and as mysterious as one, too, because I couldn't see him. He was somewhere to my right. I heard a chair scrape across the floor. He was sitting down, I figured.

"The name's Victor," he told me. "Hope you don't mind if I keep you company."

He had no way of knowing if I minded or not. If I'd had the voice to say so I probably would have told him I wanted to be alone. But the truth was, I was glad he was there.

I don't know why Victor started coming to visit me. He never let me see his face, and sometimes he didn't even talk. But just knowing he was sitting there made me feel good, and when he did talk, his words were like warm bathwater to me. I'm sounding crazy again. But if you think about it, you'll get what I mean. My life was like one big ache, and the sound of Victor's voice was the only thing that made the ache go away.

It wasn't just the sound, though; it was the stories he told me. They were all about me. Well, not about me really. They were stories he made up about someone named Cody. In some of the stories Cody was thirteen, which was what I was going to be in a couple of months if I lived that long, and he'd be doing neat stuff like exploring caves or riding the waves on his surfboard or building his own camera.

In the other stories, Cody was older. He told me about the time Cody learned to drive a car and the time he scored the winning points for his varsity basketball team and the first time he fell in love. I don't know if it showed on my face, but that last one had me blushing inside.

Victor told me stories about Cody and his kids and even his grandchildren. It was weird; when Victor wasn't around, I had trouble believing I'd make it to my thirteenth birthday, but listening to him talk, I could honestly picture myself as an eighty-year-old man.

My favorite story was the one about the time Cody went mountain climbing. That's something I always wanted to do. Victor must have taken two hours to tell me that story. He made it so real, I felt the rope burning the palms of my hands and got dizzy imagining the sheer wall of rock above me. When Cody reached the top, I felt my own heart pounding inside my chest as if it was bursting to get out.

Victor didn't usually say anything after he'd finished telling a story, but that night he did. "Someday you'll climb a mountain like that," he told me, "and you'll be surprised how much easier it's going to be than the mountain you're climbing right now."

I didn't understand what he meant then. It wasn't until after my thirteenth birthday that it made sense.

I got a whole bunch of presents for my birthday. Max stayed late and opened all of them while my mother wrote down who they were from. Max kept saying things like, "Hey, cool tape," or "Cody'll really like this shirt." And my mom would comment on how nice it was of this person or that person to remember me. My dad didn't say a word until they were all through, and then he said what I'd been thinking all along, "How in the heck do people think Cody's going to use any of this stuff?" And then I could hear some sniffling, and my dad's voice changed, and I heard him say, "I'm sorry,

Max. People mean well, but it was crazy to give Cody all this. Why don't you take it home with you?" And that was when Max really let loose and my mom, too, and they had themselves a good cry. But not my dad. I could hear his silence loudest of all.

After a while the room got quiet again, and I heard my mom say, "Now where did that come from? I didn't see anyone bring that one in, did you, Brad?" And my father said, "Sure is big." "And so beautifully wrapped," my mother added. "Someone must have left it here before we arrived. Why, it's so light."

"Is there a card?" asked Max.

There was a moment's silence. My mom was looking, I guess. "No," she said. But I was sure I knew who it was from.

Then came the sound of paper being rustled and torn, and suddenly the air in the room changed. You know how it is when you've been having a good time with a bunch of your friends and everybody's laughing and all of a sudden somebody says something really mean and stupid and everybody stops talking and you can feel the air change. *Really* feel it. That's what I felt, but I didn't know why.

Until my father said, "Of all the cruel—"

"It's probably a mistake," said my mother.

My dad said, "The box is empty, Joan. This is no mistake. It's a trick, or maybe somebody's trying to make some kind of statement."

"Statement?" my mother asked. "I don't understand."

"Who knows?" My dad's voice was going up the scale. It rises when he gets angry, like mercury in a thermometer that's heating up and you wonder if it's going to blow out the top. "'Empty life.' 'Nothing to live for.' Who knows?"

"Well, we'll just ask at the desk if any of the nurses saw anyone leave this and if not, if not..." My mother's voice faded away, the way I'd heard it do so often in the past few months.

"I say we throw it out," my father snapped.

"Can't we just leave everything in the closet tonight?" Max asked. "Maybe there's a reason—"

"Yes, yes, all right." My father's voice was loud but as empty inside as the mysterious birthday present.

Why had Victor done it?

That's what I kept asking myself all night. When he came and sat down next to me, he never said a word about it. Never said, "Hope you liked my present," or anything. But then if he'd meant to give me an empty box what *would* he say? "Hope you liked the big fat nothing I gave you for your birthday"?

I don't remember anything Victor did say that night. I'm pretty sure he told me a Cody story, but who could concentrate? All I could think about was the empty box. And the more I thought about it, the madder I got. My dad had been right, it was cruel. The problem was, I just couldn't picture Victor being cruel. He must have had a reason.

His voice went on and on, but it didn't soothe me the way it usually did. It made me want to yell at him instead, to tell him to shut up, or to say, "Stop talking about things that don't matter!"

Finally, he stopped talking. And then, in a voice so soft I might have been dreaming it, he said, "Happy birthday, Cody."

It's hard to describe what happened next. You'd have to have been inside my life then—my life of faceless Victor and his nighttime visits, and a ceiling full of nameless companions, and a closet full of useless birthday presents, and an empty box—to understand what it was like to feel myself straining upward, using every muscle to climb up out of the darkness I'd been living in, up to the Land Above, up to the top of the mountain, up to Victor.

I wasn't moving at all, of course—at least, not that anyone outside me could see. But inside me, well, inside me everything was in motion, everything was working to make one little word come out of my mouth.

"Why?"

It took a long time before Victor whispered, "Good for you, boy."

I forced the word out of me again: "Why?"

I felt his hand on mine, for the first—and, as it turned out, the last—time ever. "Well, the way I figure it," he said, "you'll be needing a box to take your things home in."

I don't remember what happened after that. I fell exhausted into a deep sleep. I dreamed that night about the Land Above. Everyone was packing as if they were going somewhere, but when I asked where, they didn't answer. They just kept saying, "It's time to move on." Only the old man was staying, and he wouldn't speak at all. I tried to get him to talk, but it was no use. Just before I woke up, I looked into his kind, ragged old face and said, "Goodbye, Victor."

The next afternoon, both my parents came. They hardly talked. When they did, their voices were like autumn leaves, dry and dusty and old. Later, Max stopped by.

"Please," I heard my dad say to him, "take this stuff, Max. Cody would want you to have it."

"What about the box?" Max asked.

"Oh, that. We'll throw it away."

That's when the feeling came over me again. I began climbing, pulling myself up. It was a little easier this time, rising, reaching for a single word: "No."

I heard my mother gasp, and Max yelled, "Cody!" They all ran to me. I saw their faces. My father's tears fell on me, rain bringing me to life again.

I never did find out for sure who Victor was. The nurses said there was an old man who walked the halls at night. His name wasn't Victor, though. And he died a couple of days after my thirteenth birthday. Whoever Victor was, he was good at miracles. And he sure knew a lot about me. He knew I'd explore caves and climb mountains. He knew I'd grow up and grow old. And he knew what I needed more than anything for my thirteenth birthday was an empty box to fill.

Promises

· Ellen Conford ·

This is the diary Laura gave me for my birthday. It probably didn't cost very much, but it's the thought that counts, they say. And at least she gave me something, which is more than certain people did.

I got a lot of better presents, too. Melanie gave me perfume, which my mother says I'm too young for, especially perfume named Sinful. Sarah gave me a CD of *Penny Dreadful's Greatest Hits.* I got plenty of good stuff.

So I'm not going to sit around and brood about why Tracy would do such a rotten thing to me, who has been her best friend since second grade.

I'm not going to waste my time going over and

over that *extremely embarrassing* moment when I opened this gorgeously wrapped box in front of everybody. How I saved it for last because it was the biggest and looked the most expensive, and I knew it just had to be something super because no one would waste all that silver paper and blue satin ribbon and huge bow with curlicues all around on a junky gift.

I can't figure Tracy out, and I'm not even going to try. Melanie said maybe she forgot to put the present in the box, but that doesn't make sense. I mean, there's this big white box, and you wrap it and pick it up and you don't notice that it doesn't weigh anything? You don't notice that the gift that's supposed to be inside is still sitting there next to the Scotch tape and scissors?

She did it on purpose, and no matter what Melanie says, everyone at the party knew it. They couldn't stop talking about it.

Well, I'm not going to spend the next two weeks of my life, till she gets back from California, wondering why she did it, but I am definitely not going to forget that she humiliated me at my own birthday party.

I don't know what satisfaction she could have gotten out of this stunt, since she wasn't even around to see my reaction. She was on the way to the airport when she dropped off the present. Come to think of it, she didn't even seem that disappointed about missing my party.

I just figured she was excited about visiting her father. She hasn't seen him since the summer, and I know she misses him.

How could I not know? She's always moaning about it. She can be so *tedious*. You'd think she was the only kid in the world whose parents ever got divorced.

I try to make her feel better by pointing this out. "Tracy," I say, "you're not the only kid in the world whose parents are divorced. Snap out of it already. It's been a year."

And she says, "You don't understand. You never understand."

Well, I don't know what she means, since it's my shoulder she's cried on since second grade, and if I don't understand, why doesn't she find somebody else's shoulder to cry on?

Though that's easier said than done. Probably the main reason I'm Tracy's best friend is because she doesn't make friends very easily. She never did. She's the quiet type. The opposite of me.

And I'm not all touchy and supersensitive like

she is. I don't make mountains out of molehills. If I had done this to *her*, she *would* sit around and brood for two weeks. She'd go over it and over it, trying to figure out how she'd hurt my feelings, or what she'd done to make me angry. She'd ask all my other friends if they knew why I was mad at her, and she wouldn't be able to think about anything else until I came home.

The least little thing upsets her.

For instance, the time I forgot about the movie we'd planned to go to.

I went to the mall that Saturday morning, and I ran into Jessica and Sarah, and we started wandering around, and then we got hungry, so we stopped at the Yogurt Hut, where this boy works that Jessica sort of likes. So we hung out there for a while, and all of a sudden I realized it was two o'clock and my mother and I were supposed to pick up Tracy at twelve-thirty.

Well, the very instant I remembered, I ran straight to the nearest phone, which wasn't even that near—I had to walk halfway through the mall to get to it—and called Tracy.

"Diane, you promised," she said. "I was looking forward to that movie all week."

"I'm sorry, Trace. I just forgot."

"You forget a lot of things," she said. "A lot of things I care about."

"Oh, come on, Tracy," I said. "It's just a movie. Don't make a huge major deal out of it."

"It's not just a movie," she said, "it's the whole—"

Then the operator cut in to say I had to deposit another dime. But I didn't see any point in staying on the phone if all Tracy wanted to do was complain about my alleged faults, so I said, "Haven't got any more change. Talk to you later."

Jessica and Sarah wanted to see the movie, so I went with them. It was really good.

Then there was last year's social studies project. Okay, that was a little more serious than a silly old movie, but still, when you think about all the truly terrible things in the world, not getting your social studies project done on time is hardly a major tragedy.

Tracy and I were partners on the project, which was due the Monday after Thanksgiving weekend. We were studying advertising claims. It was Tracy's idea, so of course she was a lot more interested in it than I was. Basically I only agreed to be her partner because I knew she didn't have a whole lot of friends to choose a partner from.

Anyway, she made a list of TV commercials and the products we would test—paper towels, toothpaste, sugarless gum, spaghetti sauce, stuff like that. She said she'd do most of the testing and that I should only do three items because I would do practically all the work on the chart and the display.

Well, it's true, I'm much more artistic than Tracy—she can hardly even draw a smiley face—but a big display like that is a whole lot of work. And even though we had four weeks for the project, Tracy only got the test results to me a week before Thanksgiving. She said she would have gotten the results to me sooner if I had done the tests I said I would do, but I pointed out that since I was doing all the work on the display, it was only fair for her to do most of the tests.

"But Diane, I had to do *all* of the tests. Even though you promised to do the gum and the paper towels and the batteries. If you'd said right at the beginning you wouldn't do them—"

"I meant to do them," I told her. "I just didn't have time."

"Four weeks wasn't enough time to do three comparison tests?" she asked sarcastically.

"Some people," I said, just as sarcastically, "have

more things to do with their lives than chew gum and wait for batteries to die."

"Some people," she said, "shouldn't make promises they don't mean to keep."

Well, that was totally unfair, because I didn't plan to *not* do the testing. It's just that a lot of other things came up, and I didn't get to it.

Anyway, even though she got me the test results at the very last minute, I had all the stuff ready to make the display—the Magic Markers, the colored pencils, the poster board. I was sure I could finish the project over the weekend.

In fact, I was already working on the chart the day after Thanksgiving when Melanie called. She was so excited I could hardly understand what she was saying.

But I was able to make out, "Uncle's ski chalet...Vermont...my folks said I could invite some friends...Laura and Jessica...real spur-of-the-moment trip...leaving in two hours...going to be so great!"

Well, I'd already started the chart, and how long could it take? We'd get home Sunday afternoon, in plenty of time to finish the display by Monday morning. Even if I had to stay up all Sunday night, it would be worth it. How could I say no?

I'd never been to a ski chalet. I'd never been to Vermont. In fact, I'd never been on skis. I knew I didn't have the right stuff to wear, but Melanie said that didn't matter. It was all going to be very country and casual, and we'd toast marshmallows in the fireplace and tromp through the snow.

She made the weekend sound like a Christmas card come to life. Nobody in their right mind would say, "Sorry, I'd really like to, but I have this social studies project to do."

Was it my fault that there was a major snowstorm that paralyzed all of New England Sunday morning? I'm not God. *I* didn't make it snow so hard that we couldn't get out of Vermont until Monday afternoon. How could Tracy blame *me* for the weather?

And it's not my fault that Ms. Brisco is so unreasonable that she wouldn't cut us an inch of slack, even though our project was two days late because of an Act of God.

Besides, it's not as if we didn't get any credit at all for the project. We just got two grades knocked off for being two days late.

"Empty promises!" Tracy screamed. "I am really fed up with your empty promises. I can't depend on you for *anything*."

She didn't speak to me for two weeks, which

was actually sort of a relief, to tell the truth. I mean, she is so self-centered. The only important problems are her problems. Nobody's interests matter as much as hers.

I don't know why I stay friends with her. I guess because I feel sorry for her, but what kind of a basis for friendship is that? And because our mothers are friends, and my mom always nags me to include Tracy in everything.

But after this rotten joke—if it is a joke—even my mother will have to admit that there's no reason to stay friends with her anymore. What possible excuse can there be for giving your best friend an empty box at her party? It would have been better if she'd just ignored my birthday completely.

No one at the party would have noticed if there was no present from her. Nobody notices Tracy anyway, and her name wouldn't have even come up this afternoon if she hadn't—

Maybe that's it. Maybe she was trying to get attention. She's always been jealous of me, I guess because she sort of fades into the woodwork when I'm around. But is it my fault that she has no personality? Can I help it if people would rather talk to me than to someone with all the spark of a stop sign?

So if I open this empty box all of a sudden, in the middle of my party, on the day of my birthday, everyone forgets about *me* and starts talking about *her.*

But if she's not even here to hear them talk about her, what can she get out of it? It doesn't make sense.

And I'm not going to waste one more minute thinking about it.

How could she be so ungrateful?

Not that I've ever expected her to thank me for all the things I've tried to do for her. Ha! That'll be the day.

Well, at least I won't have to pressure people to invite her places anymore, like my mother always wants me to. If it weren't for me, she'd never go anywhere at all. I can't count the number of times I've wangled an invitation for Tracy from someone who'd never include her in a party if I didn't insist.

And do you think she remembers all those times? Does she remember the parties I had to threaten not to go to unless she was invited?

Ha.

All she remembers is the one party I couldn't go to. And that was last July.

She was planning her birthday party. Of course

I said I would go, even though I knew it would be incredibly boring. How could it not be boring? The other kids she invited were two girls from the school Mathletes team. We were going to eat dinner at an expensive restaurant. Her father was flying in from California.

I could just imagine the evening—her mother and father hardly talking to each other, Tracy living a ridiculous fantasy about how her party would bring them back together, and the Mathletes making witty comments about algebra.

But I said I'd go.

And I would have, even though I expected it to be the longest, dullest night of my life.

Is it my fault that Tracy tells me her party is the Saturday of July Fourth weekend, and Laura tells me her party is on July fourth, and I say yes to both of them because I don't realize that they're the same day?

I mean, I don't walk around wearing a calendar on my wrist. It was a simple little mistake anybody could have made. If Tracy had sent me a written invitation like Laura did, I would have seen right away that her party was scheduled for July fourth.

Laura's party certainly sounded like a lot more fun than Tracy's. It was going to be at a country club, and she invited a lot of her brother's friends, and there would be a clambake and swimming and fireworks.

"But, Diane, you promised you'd come!" Tracy shrieked into the phone when I broke the bad news.

"I'm sorry, Trace. I got my dates mixed up."

"When did you get Laura's invitation?" she demanded. "I asked you weeks ago."

"Well, that's not really the point," I said.

"It *is* the point," she said. "I asked you first, and you said you'd come. Now you're ditching me because you think Laura's party will be better."

"Why can't you just switch your party to another day?" I suggested. "I mean, there's only the two math nerds and us and your folks. Laura's having thirty people, and they had to rent the country club. Hey! Maybe I can get her to invite you, too!"

"My father already bought his plane ticket," she said. "It's the only day he can come. And I don't want to celebrate Laura's birthday instead of my own."

"Tracy, you won't even miss me," I said. "And you won't get any less presents, because I've already bought you a *terrific* one."

I hadn't, really, but I swore to myself that I'd

buy her something extra special to make up for not going to her party.

"You think all I care about are the presents?" she yelled. "I only invited three people to my party. How could I not miss one of them?"

"I'm really, really sorry, Tracy, but it can't be helped. It's just one of those things."

"It's just one of those things that you're always doing to me," she said. Her voice was kind of tight and thin, like she had a sore throat. I hoped she wasn't going to cry.

"I said I'm sorry, Tracy. What more do you expect?"

I heard her take a deep breath. "I don't expect anything from you. Except empty promises."

"Empty prom—"

But she'd already hung up.

Laura's party was great, like I knew it would be. (And I must say I bought her a *much* more expensive present than this dinky old diary she gave me.) (No offense, Diary!) But her party did cost a whole lot more than mine did, so I guess it balances out.

Tracy started to hang out with the two math nerds who went to her party, and I haven't seen that much of her for the past few months.

In fact, if my mother hadn't insisted, I wouldn't

have asked her to my party, and she wouldn't have given me that empty box and embarrassed me in front of all my *real* friends.

Although I'm not so sure now about how real those friends are. They've been calling all evening, saying, "Oh, wasn't that weird what Tracy did?" and "How embarrassing for you," and, "You must have done something really mean to her."

They remind me of rubberneckers staring at a car accident, full of morbid curiosity.

I'm sure the minute they hang up they call each other and gossip about me and the nasty things I must have done to Tracy.

I'll have to stop for a while now. My mother wants me to get all the party junk out of the family room.

Well, I found Tracy's birthday card while we were cleaning up. It was in a mess of torn wrapping paper under a chair. It must have fallen off the package.

It's not even a real birthday card. There's a photograph of daisies on the front, and inside it says, "Friends are the flowers in the meadow of life." Isn't that icky?

Underneath that, Tracy wrote, "This present

is just like your promises. Happy birthday."

I just looked at the card and looked at the box and wondered, *What* present? There *is* no present. The box was empty.

Isn't that bizarre?

Well, Tracy always was kind of weird. Who knows what goes on in her mind? I certainly don't. And I'm not going to waste one more minute of my time trying to figure it…

Oh.

The Empty Box

· Johanna Hurwitz ·

February 17

Natures Wonder & Co.

To Whom It May Concern:

Two weeks ago I ordered the "tadpole in a bottle" kit advertised in your catalog. The package arrived yesterday, just in time for my son Jason's twelfth birthday, which was today. I didn't open your package to check it. Why should I? I had no reason to suspect that the tadpole wouldn't be inside. I covered your brown cardboard box with gift wrap and presented it to Jason this morning.

Jason ripped the paper off the box with great

anticipation. He pulled out all the Styrofoam popcorn that was inside. The kitchen floor was covered with that awful stuff, but as it was Jason's birthday, I didn't scold him. However, within a minute the whole family stood ankle deep in the Styrofoam, and it was clear that there had been a packing error on your part. There was no bottle, with or without a tadpole, inside the package. You sent an empty box!

Of course Jason was very disappointed. It's a mean trick to give an empty box to a child on his birthday. I've explained to Jason that you must have accidentally forgotten to include his bottle and that you will ship it to him immediately. I tried phoning your 800 number all afternoon, but the line has been busy. I assume that this means your business is booming and not that your phone was off the hook. I would never have guessed so many people wanted to own tadpoles. Jason is anxiously awaiting his bottle.

Sincerely,
Lillian Peacock
(Jason's mother)

February 22

Dear Valued Customer:

We regret the slight delay in sending the article you ordered.

Please expect it within the next four to six weeks.

Natures Wonder & Co.

February 23

Natures Wonder & Company

Dear Sirs:

Re: Tadpole in a bottle kit #574-10937

Some time ago, my wife ordered a tadpole kit from your firm. Your company sent an empty box to our home. It had been ordered for our son's birthday, and we shared his upset that he had been given an empty box on this special occasion.

On February 17th, my wife wrote to complain

about this error. Today, another package came from your company. Jason opened it eagerly. We were both distressed that he was faced with a second disappointment. You sent him an empty bottle! Had there been liquid in the bottle, we might have suspected that the infant tadpole was so tiny that the human eye could not yet see it. However, the bottle was totally empty. No tadpole could have existed in it.

I insist that you air-express a replacement kit to our address at once.

Yours truly,
A. Peacock

February 28

Dear Sir:

I regret to inform you that Natures Wonder & Company cannot supply you with a peacock or its eggs. However, if you consult the enclosed catalog you will see that we have chicken and duck eggs at very reasonable prices. In fact, there is an *early spring special* of twelve fertilized chicken eggs at half the usual cost.

Please fill out the enclosed order form or place your order by calling our 800 number.

We are glad to be of service to you.

Sincerely,
Ellen George
Asst. Sales Manager

P.S. We are negotiating with a new distributor and hope in the future to also be able to supply turtle eggs.

March 1

Natures Wonder & Co.

Dear Mr. Natures,

When my class studied about writing letters, I told my teacher Mrs. Shea that all my friends lived nearby. I didn't think I would ever have to bother writing a real letter. Mrs. Shea said everyone needs to write a letter at some time or other. I guess she is right because now I am writing to you.

My birthday was on February 17. It was a pretty good day. I got some neat stuff, and Mom made my favorite dinner, which is sloppy joes. The present I most wanted and kept talking about was a tadpole in a bottle kit. I really was hoping to get it. When I opened my presents I saved the biggest package for last, because I was sure that the tadpole in a bottle would be inside.

Well guess what? The box was empty (unless you count all that junk you put in a package to keep the stuff inside from breaking). My dog got sick eating all that plastic stuff. But that's not the worst thing. I am worried about my tadpole. Where is it? It wasn't in the empty bottle you sent either.

Please look for it at your company and send it to my home right away. I want to watch the tadpole turn into a frog. If you don't hurry it will be too late.

Your friend,
Jason Peacock

March 2

Natures Wonder & Company

To Whom It May Concern:

Since you have still not sent the "tadpole in a bottle" kit that I ordered more than a month ago, I am forced to write to you again. Let me remind you, I am the mother of the twelve-year-old boy who thought he was getting a "tadpole in a bottle" for his birthday. My son has been very disappointed, not only because he did not receive this gift but because of your carelessness—sending an empty package to our home.

Jason is quite mature for his age, and he understands that no one is perfect. I told him that his frog, I mean tadpole, will be arriving any day now. But am I right? Please don't make a liar out of me. Restore a young boy's faith, and send the "tadpole in a bottle" kit to our home at once.

Thank you for taking care of this.

Sincerely,
Lillian Peacock
(Mrs. Andrew Peacock)

March 5

Natures Wonder & Co.

Dear Ms. Ellen George:

Re: Tadpole in a bottle kit #574-10937

This is my last warning that if you don't immediately send a tadpole in a bottle kit to our home, I shall contact the Better Business Bureau. I hate to think how many other people, in addition to my young son, have been disappointed by the inefficient packaging done by your company. I don't know why you think I would want to order chicken eggs from you. They are easily available by the dozen at my local supermarket.

Yours truly,
A. Peacock

March 7

Dear Valued Customer:

We regret the slight delay in sending the article you ordered.

Please expect it within the next four to six weeks.

Natures Wonder & Co.

March 8

Dear Mr. Peacock:

I am responding to your letter of March 5th, which was addressed to Ms. Ellen George. Unfortunately, Ms. George no longer works here at Natures Wonder & Company. I have been promoted to her job and hope that I will be able to take care of any problems that you have.

As you know, the goal of Natures Wonder & Company is to bring the wealth and glory of the natural world into the average home. Our company specializes in selling live animals, as well as numerous products such as jewelry and clothing that take their design from the animal form.

I understand that you are interested in frogs. To this end, I have underlined in red ink all those items in our catalog that were inspired by these charming creatures. You may be especially interested in the pair of coffee mugs shaped like frogs on page 17 of our catalog. The mugs come in frog green or toad brown and hold eight ounces of beverage. The ceramic exteriors of the mugs resemble the scales on the skin of these wonderful amphibians.

In view of the problems you seem to have had when ordering from our company in the past, I wish to extend to you a one-time-only discount of 10% when you order these mugs.

Sincerely,
Marilyn Pippin
Asst. Sales Manager
Natures Wonder & Company

March 10

Natures Wonder & Co.

Dear Mr. Wonder:

I was supposed to get a tadpole in a bottle kit for my birthday last month. I have been waiting for it for a long time. I'm worried that if you don't hurry and send it to my home, the tadpole will already be a frog. Then I won't be able to watch how it grows. I heard it was a very educational experience and I don't want to miss it.

Please hurry and send my tadpole.

Your friend,
Jason Peacock

P.S. How does the frog get out of the bottle?

March 11

Natures Wonder & Company

Attention: Marilyn Pippin

Congratulations on your promotion. However, if I were you, I'd look for a job at another company. For the past month, my wife and I have written to your company repeatedly. We are not interested in peacock, chicken, or duck eggs. We certainly do not want drinking mugs that resemble frogs or toads.

On February 2nd, my wife ordered a "tadpole in a bottle" kit for our son as a birthday present. First we received an empty box. Then we received an empty bottle. Is it too much to expect a box with a tadpole in a bottle to arrive before our son's next birthday?

I have threatened before to inform the Better Business Bureau about the sloppy manner in which your firm conducts its operation. Please know that I am sending them a duplicate copy of this letter. I do not want other children to have the same disappointment on their birthday that my son had.

Yours truly,
A. Peacock

March 18

Dear Mr. Peacock,

I know you will be disappointed to hear that Natures Wonder & Company has decided to discontinue shipping live tadpoles in bottles to its customers. We now plan to limit our stock to stuffed frogs (made out of cloth, not real frog), ceramic frogs, frog posters, and a large and unusual stone frog, which can be used as a garden seat.

In view of the problems you have had in the past weeks in trying to obtain a "tadpole in a bottle" kit for your son, I have arranged that the company ship all remaining stock of such bottles to your address. I'm sorry they won't arrive in time for your son's birthday—either this year's or next—but I know that young boys are delighted to get gifts at any time of the year.

Most sincerely,
Marilyn Pippin
Sales Manager
Natures Wonder

April 1

Natures Wonder & Co.

Dear Mr. Natures Wonder,

This has been the best day of my life. It's spring break so I was home from school when the United Parcel truck came to my house this morning. The driver brought two big boxes, and they were addressed to *me*. Then he went back to his truck and brought two more. All together there were twenty-four boxes!

Underneath those plastic pieces that you put in the boxes to keep the stuff inside from breaking was a tadpole in the bottle kit in each box. I never dreamed I would ever own twenty-four tadpoles. The tadpoles were pretty big. In fact, they were practically frogs. They had legs and feet and only the tiniest bit of tail left. It's too bad that I missed watching them grow up, but I don't care. It's great to have twenty-four frogs.

My friend Allan came over to my house, and very, very carefully, we broke the bottles so that the frogs could get out. At the moment they are all in my bathtub hopping about. I'm not sure how we are going to get washed. I think if we all took showers without using any soap it will work out fine.

Thanks a lot for sending all the frogs. I know I'm going to learn a lot just watching them.

Your friend,
Jason Peacock

P.S. Do dogs eat frogs? I hope not.

P.P.S. If my mother says I can't keep them all, I'm going to give them to my friends as birthday surprises.

Selected Bibliography

For reasons of space, the following listings of titles are only partial. These and other titles should be available at school and local libraries and at bookstores.

David A. Adler is the author of the Cam Jansen series, including *Cam Jansen and the Mystery of the Dinosaur Bones* (Puffin, 1991), and the Houdini Club Magic Mysteries, including *Wacky Jacks* (Random, 1994). He is also the author of nonfiction books, including the Picture Book Biography series (Holiday House), *We Remember the Holocaust* (Holt, 1989), and *Child of the Warsaw Ghetto* (Holiday House, 1995).

Ellen Conford is the author of *Dear Mom, Get Me Out of Here* (Little, Brown, 1993); *I Love You, I Hate You, Get Lost* (Scholastic, 1994); and the Jenny Archer series, including *Nibble Nibble, Jenny Archer* (Little, Brown, 1993) and *Get the Picture, Jenny Archer?* (Little, Brown, 1994), among other titles.

Pam Conrad is the author of *Holding Me Here* (Harper, 1986), *My Daniel* (Harper, 1991), *Pedro's Journal: A Voyage with Christopher Columbus* (Scholastic, 1992), *Prairie Songs* (Harper, 1987), *Prairie Visions: The Life and Times of Solomon Butcher* (Harper, 1991), *Stonewords: A Ghost Story* (Harper, 1991), and other books.

James Howe is the author of the Bunnicula series, including the *Bunnicula Fun Book* (Morrow, 1993) and *Return to Howliday Inn* (Atheneum, 1992); the Sebastian Barth mysteries, including *Dew Drop Dead* (Atheneum, 1990); *The Hospital Book* (Morrow, 1994); *A Night Without Stars* (Atheneum, 1983); and other titles.

Johanna Hurwitz is the author of *A Llama in the Family* (Morrow, 1994) and the Class Clown series, including *Class Clown* (Morrow, 1987), *Class President*

(Morrow, 1990), *School's Out* (Morrow, 1991), *School Spirit* (Morrow, 1994), and *Teacher's Pet* (Morrow, 1988), along with other titles.

Karla Kuskin is the author of *City Dog* (Houghton Mifflin, 1994), *Dogs and Dragons, Trees and Dreams* (Harper, 1992), *Near the Window Tree: Poems and Notes* (Harper, 1975), *Patchwork Island* (Harper, 1994), *Paul* (Harper, 1994), and *The Philharmonic Gets Dressed* (Harper, 1982), among other titles.

Ann M. Martin is the author of the Baby-sitters Club series and the Baby-sitters Little Sister series, as well as other titles for young readers, including *Ten Kids, No Pets* (Scholastic, 1989) and *Rachel Parker, Kindergarten Show-off* (Holiday House, 1992). Her next picture book, *The Amazing True Story of Leo the Magnificat,* will be published by Scholastic.

Richard Peck has written four books starring Blossom Culp: *The Ghost Belonged to Me* (Dell, 1987), *Ghosts I Have Been* (Dell, 1987), *The Dreadful Future of Blossom Culp* (Dell, 1994), and *Blossom Culp and the Sleep of Death* (Dell, 1994). Among his other books are *Voices After Midnight* (Dell, 1990) and *Bel-Air Bambi and the Mall Rats* (Dell, 1994).

Barbara Ann Porte is the author of *Fat Fanny, Beanpole Bertha, & the Boys* (Orchard, 1991); books about Harry, including *Harry's Birthday* (Greenwillow, 1994); *I Only Made Up the Roses* (Greenwillow, 1987); *Something Terrible Happened* (Orchard, 1994); *Ruthann and Her Pig* (Orchard, 1989); and books about Abigail and Sam, including *A Turkey Drive and Other Tales* (Greenwillow, 1993).

Jane Yolen is the author of *Children of the Wolf* (Puffin, 1993), *The Devil's Arithmetic* (Puffin, 1990), *Dove Isabeau* (Harcourt, 1989), *The Dragon's Boy* (Harper, 1990), *The Gift of Sarah Barker* (Puffin, 1992), and *The Girl in the Golden Bower* (Little, Brown, 1994), among other titles.